BARRY BARRISON
GHOST DETECTIVE

The Tarford Inheritance

OTHER HEXAGON COMICS
NOVELS & COLLECTIONS

BARRY BARRISON GHOST DETECTIVE

The Tarford Inheritance

By
Philippe Pinon

Adapted by
Jean-Marc Lofficier
& **Nina Cooper**

Based on the characters created by
Claudio Tiziano Fusi & Luciano Bernasconi

BLACK COAT PRESS

Acknowledgements: Thomas Guenault, David Baudet, Jim, Lester L. Gore, Romain D'Huissier, Julien Heylbroeck, Charles Griggs and Nathan Lynas.

Visit our websites at
www.blackcoatpress.com
and
www.hexagoncomics.com

TABLE OF CONTENTS

I dedicate this book to my father,
who introduced me to *Harry Dicksons* when I was 12,
and to my sweet Selene Meynier,
without whom this book would never have seen
the light of day.
P.P.

Introduction

Barry Barrison, Ghost Detective: The Tarford Inheritance is the latest in a series of novels and short story collections based on characters from the Hexagon Comics universe.

Hexagon Comics is the successor of France's Editions Lug, once the 5th largest publisher of comic magazines in that country. From 1950 to the early 1990s, Lug published a large array of monthly pocket-sized comic books, with colorful covers and titles beloved by many generations of teenagers.

While novels based on comics are not new in the United States, where novels based on *Batman* or the *X-Men* have long existed, that subgenre is virtually inexistent in France.

Originally entitled *L'Ami Barry* [Our Friend, Barry], the *Barry Barrison* comic was first published as a six-issue mini-series in 1982. It was the creation of Italian writer Claudio Tiziano Fusi and artist Luciano Bernasconi. Born in 1939 in Rome, Bernasconi started in comics in the early 1960s, and was, for over twenty years, one of the architects of Editions Lug, for which he created a large number of heroes such as *Sibilla, Phenix, Wampus, Kabur, Bob Lance, The Bronze Gladiator, Jeff Sullivan, Kit Kappa, Starlock*, and many more.

So who is Barry Barrison? He was an English lord who lived a peaceful and relatively opulent life in his stately home at Tarford Manor in London in the later part of the 19th century.

A contemporary of the great detective Sherlock Holmes, he possessed the same skills of deduction which made him one of the best amateur detectives of that era.

After being murdered in the spring of 1900, Barrison was condemned to wander about in his mansion in a ghostly form, until a group of university students comprised of Terry, his girl-friend Angela, their rich friend Mark Tarford, and his friend, the medium Maureen Simpson (whom they had just prevented from being murdered), conjured up Barry's ectoplasmic form back from limbo to help them solve the kind of mysteries that are usually beyond the police's abilities to solve.

It is unlikely that the creators of *Barry Barrison* were influenced by the 1969 British TV series *Randall and Hopkirk (Deceased)* (a.k.a. *My Partner the Ghost*), but both succeed in carrying out the basic premise of a Ghost Detective with a great deal of charm and cleverness.

Writer Philippe Pinon has scripted and acted in a few short films and is a passionate fan of role-playing games, heroic fantasy, and TV series. He had already contributed two short stories to the *Tales of the Hexagonverse* series: "The Mystery of the Woman Who Walks," included in this volume, and another about *The Agent With No Name* that will be published in our third installment, *The Others*, later this year. When he volunteered to expand the former and turn it into a full-blown *Barry Barrison* collection, I enthusiastically accepted, and you hold the result in your hand.

Now, read on…

Jean-Marc Lofficier

Terry Edwards & Angela Lake

Maureen Simpson

Mark Tarford & Maureen Simpson

The Quiet Game

1.

The driver of the hired carriage waited patiently in front of the entry to the cottage, aware of the importance of the trip to come. His client, a certain Barry Barrison, had a reputation for being somewhat demanding, but also for being someone who knew how to be generous. Higgins told himself that he had the opportunity to show how efficient his driving was. The driver secretly hoped to get a generous tip.

The door to the cottage on Essex Road finally opened and a man with fair skin, and of excellent height, wearing a fashionable suit, came out of it. He was leaning nonchalantly on a finely-crafted walking cane. He motioned to the driver with a nod, closed the door behind himself, readjusted his high hat and stepped toward the carriage. Higgins opened the door as he greeted his client.

"17 Regent Street, please," said Barry Barrison, taking a seat in the carriage.

"Certainly, Sir," Higgins answered.

After having closed the door, Higgins jumped onto his carriage seat and took up the reins of his team. The horses started with a trot toward Westminster. Seated comfortably at the rear, Barry began to reflect, his gaze lost in the distance, following God alone knew what thoughts. His blue-gray eyes shone with intense light, a sign that he was in deep thought. About forty, the aristocrat refused to accept the life of leisure that his good fortune had been able to bring him. He needed to keep his brain occupied, or he would die of boredom, according to his own words.

He placed his hat on the vacant seat beside him, and took out a letter from his inside pocket. He unfolded it and read the missive once again, stroking his thin mustache.

My very dear friend,

I know that your time is precious. I therefore wouldn't ask for your help if the situation were not of unusual urgency, at least in my opinion.

During the time that we have known each other, you know how logical I am by nature, and not prone to believe in all sorts of strange ideas, in whatever appearance they may be clothed. Frequently, during all those years we have known each other, you have only reinforced my inner conviction that the world is a logic and rational place. In all our conversations exchanged in the course of these last years, there is at least one obvious fact that stands out: You wouldn't be so often compared to the Great Detective himself if your deductive abilities were in the least questionable. You can also be sure that I wouldn't have revealed to you so many details about my business if I didn't have entire confidence in you. Finally, among all your superlative attributes, the one that irritates me the most is your excellence in the noble game of chess.

That said, I must now admit the unthinkable. I believe I am losing my mind. I can no longer remember certain facts. At Tarford Manor, Alfred, my butler, swore that he told me more than once certain facts of which I have no memory. At Tree's, my club, I had conversa-

tions, about which any details escape me. I have been seen by some of my neighbors taking my daily walk in Hyde Park, when I thought I was writing, alone, in my study. I find things in one place when I am sure I left them in another. And what can I say about doors that I find closed, when I am sure that I left them open.

In short, as I'm sure you will understand, I need your powers. Am I in the process of slowly stumbling into madness? Have I been struck by the same degenerative disease that afflicted my mother so long ago? Or worse still?

Whatever the truth, I must know it, in order to react appropriately. That's why I would be indebted to you if you could find some time to come to Tarford Manor so that we could discuss my problem in detail, and you could give your verdict, whatever it may be, in confidence. There is no one else in the world that I trust more than you, not even myself. I am certain that your judgment will always be the best.

Your devoted,

Sir Henry Tarford

Barry folded the letter carefully and put it back into his pocket. From merely an acquaintance in his early days, Sir Henry had become one of his closest friends over the years. Their acquaintance had begun at a chess tournament organized by the Queen's Pawn, one of the best-known chess societies in London. Henry and he had found themselves the finalists after three whole days spent eliminating their respective adversaries, one after the other. The final game had been a memorable one. However, it had begun in a very conventional way. Barry played black. The opening with three knights was also known as *Giuoco Piano*, or *The Quiet Game*.

Barry had been expecting an adversary of middle ability, who would have boned up on the basic theories of chess openings. Besides, he had begun the encounter in a very relaxed manner, raising his play at regular intervals between each move, chatting casually with the spectators, certain of his victory. But Henry hadn't wavered... Concentrating on the board, he had managed his opening perfectly, leaving Barry no opening.

Barry became aware of the strength of his opponent at the nineteenth move, when his opponent took more than seventy minutes before playing 19Ce3, which made the crowd break into applause. From that point on, Barry's entire attention was on the game. Taking his seat again, he concentrated harder on the contest that was taking place on the chessboard. And it was only after three hours of relentless battle that Henry retired his king, stood up, shook the hand of his adversary and gave him a warm smile of congratulation.

"Sir, we have arrived."

The coachman's voice drew Barry away from his thoughts. He passed his hand over his eyes, wondered how long he had day-dreamed. He picked up his hat. Higgins opened the door, letting him out of the carriage and into the street. Barry stretched his back and took out a pound note that he placed in the hand of the driver, who, after a moment of disbelief, managed to say, "Much obliged. Thank you, Sir."

Barry had just paid more than ten times the price of a usual drive.

"You're welcome, my friend," he responded as he approached the wrought-iron gate which led into Tarford Manor. "They are a little painful for the shoulders to open!" he continued, going through the gate and disappearing from the sight of the coachman.

Before the driver was able to reply, the elegant aristocrat was already on the little stone walk that wound across the perfectly kept lawn that surrounded the large building. Realizing it was too small for his carriage to enter, Higgins again mounted his sea and gazed at the high wrought-iron fence that encircled Tarford Manor. Imposing and elegant at the same time, it protected the property from the unwanted without disfiguring the area. He took his fob watch out of his vest pocket and gave it a rapid glance, then carefully placed the one-pound note at the bottom of his pocket. Satisfied, he then put his carriage in a slow trot. His day was over.

Barry arrived at the foot of the stairs which led toward the steps. As was his habit, he was careful to avoid the sixth step, damaged since Alfred had let a big tree fall down there several months before. He grasped the large forged-iron door knocker, sculpted in the image of a wolf's head, and knocked twice on the oak door. He turned around to take advantage of the view. The garden was magnificent. The roses were all pruned in the same fashion, no weed was left, and the grass was cut short, as it should be. It was rare to see such a large garden in the heart of London. If it had not been the proximity of Westminster, Barry would have believed himself in the country.

No one came to the door. Barry knocked again, louder, and wiped his hand with a handkerchief that he took from his pocket. After several seconds, the heavy door was finally opened, revealing the frail silhouette of the old butler.

"Sir Barry!" exclaimed an overjoyed Alfred. "I am very happy to see you! Please come in. Let me take your coat. I didn't hear you," he continued, adjusting the little square glasses pushed up on his forehead. "I was in the kitchen, preparing a sauce for Sir Henry's dinner. I was at the point of peeling the onions..."

Barry smiled at the old butler, whose gray curls were becoming thin on his skull. However, Alfred still had that same sharp look that Barry had spotted in him years ago. His silhouette had become a little thinner, certainly, but the affability of the butler erased his apparent aging.

"Please, my dear Alfred," Barry answered in a happy voice, "I know how much you excel in the preparation of your culinary accomplishments. I apologize for having disturbed you."

"Not at all, I assure you. And you are too kind to me, Sir. But," Alfred continued, taking the overcoat and hat of his guest, "I assure you that I am not a little proud of my cooking."

He gave Barry a long look, adding, "And these days, God knows if Sir Henry needs good meals! He has almost stopped eating, you know. In spite of all my efforts, he almost never touches his meals."

He returned after having hung up his jacket and overcoat. His eyebrows were wrinkled and a frown had formed on his wrinkled face.

"I fear that Sir Henry is really not well," he continued.

Barry put his hand on the old man's shoulder. "I know, Alfred. Sir Henry has asked me for help."

Alfred's eyes became filled with barely controlled tears. "The day before yesterday," he continued, "I even believed that Sir Henry had lost his mind."

"What do you mean?"

"Sir Henry had asked me, at the beginning of the afternoon, to go get him a new kind of tea at Emily's Emporium. I did that and I returned just in time to prepare it for him at about six o'clock. After that, I got ready to take it to him. It seemed to me that I heard a rather loud conversation in his office, then a dull sound. I went to the coat hook to check if there were any clothes left by a visitor, but there was none. I remained mystified for a moment, asking myself what I should do. I went quietly down the corridor leading to the office. The voices continued, but were no longer but a soft whisper. I very quickly returned to the kitchen where I had left the tea and hurried again toward the office. I was nervous and my hands trembled so much that the saucer shook on the platter. I knocked. When I heard, '*Come in, Alfred,*' I admit that I let out a great sigh of relief."

The old man paused.

"I hurried to open the door, fearing to see Sir Henry in an excited state, but he was, on the contrary, quite calm, but with his gaze somewhat unfocused. He greeted me with a big smile and motioned for me to put the platter on his desk. That's what I did, without saying anything."

Alfred shook his head. "I admit that I was very concerned."

Barry had listened to the old butler's story with a great deal of attention. He smiled at the old man. "Have no fear, Alfred, everything will turn out well."

The old butler's face lit up; his expression full of hope.

"You know that Sir Henry is the only person that I have left in my life. I can't imagine what I would do if I were no longer in his service. For more than forty years, I have worked for the Tarfords; forty years of good and loyal service for a family that has always treated me with perfect courtesy. Even if I didn't have the honor of knowing Lady Tarford very long, she was a remarkable woman, very attentive and affectionate toward Sir Henry."

He swallowed painfully. "I don't know what has been troubling Sir Henry for several days now, but it's serious, I'm certain of it. I'm glad that he has called on you. If there is one person whom he trusts, it's you Sir Barry."

Barrison put his hand in that of the old butler. "Count on me, Alfred," he answered gently. "I'm going to talk with Sir Henry. Afterward, we will see what has to be done. But do as I ask, will you?"

"Of course!" the butler replied. "But why do you ask that?"

"Go rest; you need it very much."

"I, rest? But... why do you say that?"

Barrison winked at him: "Because I know; Alfred, I know."

And without giving the old butler time to answer, Barry started down the wide corridor which led to the main sitting room, filled with a diverse and varied collection of objects, some protected under glass. Alfred watched him walk away. Putting his hand on his painful back, he was very happy that Barry Barrison was here. If there was one man who could get his master out of that situation, it was certainly he.

2.

Barry opened the French door that led to the main drawing room. The end-of-the-afternoon sun flooded the vast room. The aristocrat advanced two steps and closed the heavy door behind him carefully.

"Hello, Henry!" he threw out in a tone that he hoped was the most carefree possible. His gaze was fixed on the big Louis XV chair which was like a throne in the left section of the drawing room, facing the chess-board. His friend was sitting there, as he usually did, his eyes fixed on a game in progress. Older than Barrison, Sir Henry Tarford had the upright bearing of the English aristocrat, without being the perfect caricature of it. His perfectly trimmed beard, as well as his graying side-burns, gave his long face an apparent air of wisdom which none of his acquaintances denied. He was dressed in a perfectly cut gray suit, wearing a dazzling white shirt, the cuffs of which were held together with cuff-links bearing the family arms. His joined hands rested under his chin, and his gaze was fixed on the board, which featured a variation on a game with four knights and a king's pawn, the same combination that had sealed his friendship with Barry years before.

Barry's smile faded quickly, however. Despite the prodigious heat from the sun's rays, a breath of cold air made him shiver. He noticed tiny drops of sweat on his friend's forehead. He approached the easy chair and put his hand on Sir Henry's shoulder.

"Henry?"

The man jumped. He turned his head toward Barry. Finally emerging from his reverie, he rose to hug his friend.

"Barry, my friend! Forgive me for having ignored you," he said with a big smile, "but I was lost in my thoughts. You know that, despite all these years playing against you and almost always losing, I still enjoy it as much as ever?"

He gently tapped on Barry's shoulder, inviting him to sit down across from him.

"Henry, don't lie to me..." Barry began.

His friend threw him a surprised look.

"You were not in the process of thinking," Barry continued, refusing the invitation to sit down.

He walked toward the French doors that opened onto the garden, and closed them.

"You don't have a glass of Armagnac nearby, and I have never seen you play without it. What's more, your sleeves are down and the cufflinks are in place. You may have been expecting me, but if you were truly relaxing, you would have gotten comfortable before sitting down. You know as well as I do that lowered cuffs aren't very practical for those who give themselves to the noble game. The risk of having to resort to *adoubement*[1] is too frequent."

Barry returned toward the board. His gaze swept the pieces. Sir Henry moved toward the fireplace on the other side of the room. He picked up a poker and mechanically stirred up the half-cold ashes.

"What's more, you have played," Barry continued. "Badly, certainly, but you have already played. That proves without the shadow of a doubt that you are not yourself."

"Because I forgot that I had played?"

"No, Henry, because you played so badly. That is not like you, most of all, so soon in a game."

Sir Henry placed the poker against the side of the fireplace and returned toward his friend. He let himself collapse, more than he sat down, on a chair. He stayed silent for long seconds. Barry went toward the liquor cabinet, took two glasses and the carafe of Armagnac of magnificent age that was placed on a finely chiseled silver platter. He took the time to observe his friend. Sir

---

[1] The act of putting a chess piece in place without playing it. (Note from the author.)

Henry had a furrowed brow and an ashy complexion. From all appearances, he had not enjoyed a good night's sleep in a while. He who ordinarily overflowed with energy, seemed at the end of his rope, as cold as the ashes in the fireplace. Barry filled two glasses with Armagnac and slid one onto the low table in front of his friend. He picked up the other one and sat down in front of his friend.

On a wall a grandfather clock was sounding the seconds.

"Tell me everything that I don't already know, Henry," he finally said, crossing his legs.

Sir Henry sighed unhappily. He picked up the glass and took a large swallow.

"What do you already know, my friend?"

"That you must spare Alfred. The poor man can't go on like this any longer," Barrison answered.

"Alfred? But what is the connection? And why do you say that?"

"There is no direct connection, except that Alfred is too devoted to you, and in these troubled times, his daily presence could only prove to be an appreciable comfort to you."

"Certainly, my friend, but I still don't understand..."

"How would you feel if your butler had to be confined to bed because he found himself in such a state of fatigue that he could no longer provide his services?"

Sir Henry turned pale.

"It's as bad as that? I knew that I was asking a lot of him lately, but I was far from imagining that he was on the verge of collapse."

"He is. His shoulder is painful. He has difficulty getting around. His arthritis causes him to suffer painfully."

"His arthritis? But how..."

Barry put down his glass without having drunk from it.

"The sixth step."

Faced with the inquiring gaze of his friend, Barry explained.

"Those stairs that lead into your house have been broken for weeks. Alfred, usually so prompt to repair the least thing, has still not done anything to fix them."

"Perhaps he hasn't had the time?"

"No, my friend, it has nothing to do with time. It's a necessary task that requires precision. And with a trembling arthritic hand, it's impossible to do that work well. He could not hold a trowel firmly enough. Alfred knows that. And rather than admit his feebleness, he prefers to ignore the issue."

"I am afraid, Barry," Sir Henry interrupted.

Despite himself, Barry felt troubled by that remark, throw out point blank.

"The tone of your letter couldn't have been more explicit," he said.

"Do you think I am losing my mind?"

"No, my friend. You are as sane as I am."

"And that's supposed to reassure me?"

Sir Henry smiled in an unexpected burst of mischievousness, but soon became sad again.

"I don't know, Henry," said Barry. "I need more information in order to understand what is happening to you."

Sir Henry stood up, putting down his glass, which he had barely touched.

"What can I add other than what I wrote in my letter?"

Barry uncrossed his legs. He took his old tobacco pouch and his pipe with a curved stem out of his vest pocket. With a nod, he asked his host for his permission to smoke. Sir Henry gave it with a wave of his hand.

"Bring me up to date on every detail, however insignificant it may seem to you, regarding your so-called memory problems," asked Barry, methodically filling his pipe.

"What can I you say other than I seem to no longer be myself? Worse: no longer know what I am doing! You know, Barry, there is nothing more frightening than the sensation of no longer being yourself."

Barry lit his pipe and drew in several intakes of white, odorous smoke until the fire in the pipe seemed right to him. After a few seconds, he exhaled, sending out a cloud of perfumed smoke.

"Your daily walks, have they always taken place at the same time?"

"Almost always, yes." Sir Henry confirmed. "At the end of the afternoon."

"And when your neighbors saw you walking about, when you thought that you were writing in your study, do you know what time it was?"

"Alfred had just served me tea; so it was about 6 o'clock."

"Have you talked to those people after that incident?"

"No, not since then."

"When was that?"

"Only a few days later; less than a week, in any case."

"Why did you believe their statements without checking them? Weren't you curious to do so? If someone had seen me in one place, when I wasn't aware of being there, you can be sure that I would have tried to interrogate these witnesses in order to get as many details as I could."

Sir Henry moved about on his seat and made an annoyed gesture.

"I'm sorry, Barry, if I don't have the same rigor as you!" he replied, exasperated. "I don't conduct a lengthy investigation of everything when I am busy doing something else. But you are right. I should have questioned my neighbors. However, I admit that the fear of exposing a truth that would only upset me more, took precedence over all the rest!"

Barry observed his friend. Having known him for years, he had learned to understand Henry Tarford. Since their memorable first game, at the finale of the Queen's Pawn Tournament, a deep friendship had existed between them, one that didn't need words to be expressed. What was bothering him now was that Henry was not being his usual prolix self when telling his story, and less than demonstrative in the sentiments that he was expressing. The conversations between the two men were often long monologues from Henry that Barry listened to with a sincere and attentive ear. One of them loved to talk and open his heart; the other to listen and analyze what he had heard. This was not the case here.

"There is some truth that bothers you? What is it?" asked Barry, exhaling a new cloud of smoke.

"The thought that I have that same sickness that took away my mother. I have lived under that Sword of Damocles hanging over my head since she passed, asking myself every day if I won't fall victim to the same disastrous fate."

Sir Henry stood up. He walked toward the chess board. Stopping in front of it, he crossed his arms and contemplated for a brief instant the wooden pieces.

"Will you help me, my friend?" he finally said

"Do you doubt it?"

"No, of course not," he replied with a sad smile. "But I had to ask."

"So that I could answer you?"

"If it's not worth the trouble."

Sir Henry sat down again, facing his friend.

"Thank you," he said in a most serious tone. "So will you accept an invitation for dinner tomorrow evening?"

"A dinner? What an idea, Henry," replied Barry, frowning. "Are you sure that this is a good time?"

His friend smiled again.

"There are no circumstances that should divide people of good will, and there are some of my friends that I have been remiss not to introduce to you."

"Alfred just told me that your appetite had become, er, more delicate."

"It is that, my friend. That is why I hope that sharing a moment of conviviality will help me forget my fears and bring me back the taste for excellent food."

Barry gave him a smile.

"So be it then, Henry!" he said rising. "Looking forward to tomorrow evening, I am going to think a little about your story, and, why not, even take a walk where you were supposedly seen without being there."

He rose and went toward the door. Sir Henry followed in his footsteps, stepping in front of him to open it. Barry suddenly stopped.

"One last thing, Henry," he said, tapping his nose with his right index finger.

"Anything you want, my friend," the other answered, inviting him with a courteous gesture to join him in the corridor

"Will you permit me to invite Father Howard?"

Sir Henry hesitated for an instant.

"Why, yes, of course, Barry… But if you will allow me, do you think the situation is so dire that you should bring a priest to my table? I have been a good friend to Father Howard, no question about it, but I can't quite grasp the reason for his presence at our dinner."

Barry placed a reassuring hand on Henry's shoulder.

"Just because he's a friend, Henry, one of your oldest friends."

"Well, er, your request does surprise me a little… But I shall welcome Father Howard among us tomorrow night. I will ask Alfred to add one more setting. Let's not talk anymore about it."

They had come to the large vestibule. Alfred appeared from an adjacent room like a jumping jack out of its box. He took Barry's coat from the rack and held it out to him. Barry put it on, thanking the butler with a nod.

"Shall we say seven, Henry?" he asked. "I will pick up Father Howard. His old legs have trouble carrying him nowadays. It'll save him a tiring walk."

"Seven will be perfect," replied Sir Henry.

He smiled at his friend, and the two men exchanged a warm handshake.

"Thanks again, and God bless you."

"I haven't done anything yet, Henry. You can thank me later. For now, I feel like a walk. And it's time to do some thinking."

After a wave at the old butler, Barry Barrison left Tarford Manor, walking with tranquil steps toward Hyde Park.

Alfred watched him for a long moment before closing the door. Then he turned around, a smile on his lips, Sir Henry had already disappeared back into the drawing room.

3.

The rain poured down on London at the beginning of the afternoon, accompanied by a wind that blew in strong waves. Seated comfortably in the carriage which carried him toward the little church where Father Howard officiated, Barry Barrison was thinking. His gaze was fixed on a file in front of him. Frowning, he was plunged in intense concentration. Since his meeting with Sir Henry the evening before, he had not ceased turning over the different information in his head, searching for a logical explanation for all of it. A sleepless night and a fire in the hearth, consumed right up to its last embers, hadn't been enough, however. And even if he had already eliminated certain possibilities, he was still lacking too many elements to allow him to lay out with certainty his profound conviction. He had to know more about the entire affair.

His stroll in Hyde Park hadn't been any help, or almost none. He had gone past the habitual strollers, who remained seated on a bench a good part of their afternoon, letting time flow by and watching people pass by. He had stopped to question some of them, describing Sir Henry in order to know if they saw him often, and if they had seen him that certain day. He received diverse and varied answers, going from: *never met him!* to *Yes,*

of course! I see him almost every day. A charming gen-
tleman who never fails to say hello, followed by answers
such as: *a lunatic if there ever was one,* or also *perhaps,*
but you must understand, I am old and I don't pay much
attention to everything that takes place around me.

Barry sighed. These diverse answers summed up
the quintessence of man: his versatility and his lack of
reliability. He had known for years that a man who
watches is one who sees the least. He had the perfect
demonstration of that that afternoon. He was snatched
out of his thoughts by the sound of his coach stopping in
a little street next to Father Howards's church. The voice
of the driver reached him from his high seat:

"Do you want me to go in and ask for the person
that we have come to get? Or will they come by themselves?"

Barry took out his pocket watch and glanced at it.
"Father Howard is punctual. Let's wait!"

"All right, Sir. Hoping that you are right about that.
It's raining cats and dogs and I'm soaked."

Barry smiled, but didn't reply. Almost immediately,
from the street corner, he spied the silhouette of Father
Howard, a jovial octogenarian still alert despite being a
tad overweight. He was in a fast trot, protecting his bald
head with a small, half-torn umbrella. He arrived near
the carriage. The coachman jumped down from his seat
and hurried to open the door. Father Howard threw himself in, out of breath. The door closed behind him. The
carriage bounced during the time that the priest was trying his best to get into a space that was obviously uncomfortable for him. Then the carriage started off again.
Barry gave a friendly nod to the priest.

"Barry Barrison!" said Father Howard. "I haven't seen you in a quite a long time. How many years is it? Four? Five? I no longer remember very well."

The priest held out his hand to the aristocrat. They exchanged a frank and warm handshake.

"Five years, as a matter of fact," Barry replied. "I admit that my own business has consumed all of my free time, and I no longer have time enough to devote myself to the good works of your parish as I did before."

Father Howard lifted his hand, signifying that he wasn't being accusatory.

"Please, don't excuse yourself, Barry. I wasn't giving you a sermon. All the years during which you brought help to me and my modest parish are sufficient proof of your good soul. You will have your place at the right hand of Our Lord—as late as possible, obviously," he continued with a smile, "but rest assured on that subject."

Then his face took on a concerned expression, frowning.

"Let's talk about that dinner invitation. What's the matter with Sir Henry? He, too, no longer comes to Church."

"How long has he been missing?"

"Two weeks at the most. Lately, I have felt that he was perturbed. He was strangely more attentive than in the past; it was obvious, but also more concerning."

The carriage continued to jostle the two men around as it took several sharp turns.

"What do you mean by *more attentive?*" Barry inquired.

"You know that for many years Sir Henry came to Sunday Mass, like most Christians, to be seen by the other members of the Parish and to avoid being criticized. There are a great number of pretenders among my flock. Just because I am a man of the cloth, I am not naive. I know how to tell the difference between a man or woman who sincerely listen to my words, and those who are there just for appearances. And during Sir Henry's recent appearances, I felt that he was a great deal more attentive than in the past."

"Do you have any idea why?"

Father Howard shook his head.

"No," he responded. "I have been tempted several times to speak to him, at the end of Mass, but he always declined, claiming he had some urgent business. That was even stranger."

The priest passed his hand over his bald head.

"Are you finally going to tell me, Barry, why you have asked me to come?"

The amateur detective crossed his legs.

"Sir Henry believes that he is losing his mind."

Father Howard opened his eyes wide, astonished.

"What? He believes he is going mad?"

"Yes, that's what he feels. He says that he is losing his memory, that he has absences…" Barry paused, scrutinizing the priest. "In short, he's afraid."

"I understand," observed Father Howard, with a nod of his head. "But how can I help him? Beyond the spiritual, I mean."

"To be candid, I don't know yet. You will probably have the opportunity to talk to him during dinner. I will make sure you're seated next to him. And you will find the right words, Father, of this, I am certain." After another pause, he continued. "What I expect of you, and this should remain between us, is that you observe Sir Henry."

Father Howard, ill at ease, squirmed on his seat.

"Observe him? What do you mean exactly?"

"Let us be clear, Father," Barry replied, noticing the embarrassment of the man of the Church. "I'm not asking you to spy on him, but to tell me if something in his behavior seems abnormal to you. Sir Henry mentions absences. I need to know, tonight, if they manifest themselves in one way or another, or if you notice something unusual in his behavior."

"Like a change in his personality? Or the beginning of insanity? An incipient descent into madness?"

Barry acquiesced, his expression serious. "You understood me precisely, Father. You are a man in whom both Sir Henry and I have entire confidence. You have known him almost from birth...

"Why, yes," cut in Father Howard. "I performed his Confirmation!"

"Quite," Barry continued. "You're one of those who know him best. I am counting on you. Every detail could be important."

"I understand, Barry, and I thank you for the trust that you've placed in me."

The priest relaxed and leaned back a little more into his seat, letting himself be bounced about by the jolts of the carriage. Outside, the rain increased in violence. The gusts of wind whipped between the houses and swept about the debris in the gutters. The branches of the trees bent over; their leaves fell and zigzagged left to right in the street like a headless chicken.

"Even so," continued Father Howard, after some thought, "this is rather sad, don't you think? Sir Henry suffered much from the passing of his mother. He deserves to end his days in peace."

"Let's not get ahead of ourselves! He is a little more than fifty... To speak of the end end of his days is somewhat of an exaggeration... Unless..."

The priest stared at Barry and his round face turned purple. Barry frowned. He uncrossed his legs and leaned over the edge of the seat. Father Howard rubbed his hands together, ill at ease.

"I see. How long have you known?" Barry asked.

The question fell like the blow of a hammer, cold and brutal.

"What... what are you talking about?" said the priest, whose embarrassment only increased.

"About his sickness."

Father Howard crossed himself, visibly relieved. He stopped rubbing his hands, and smiled sadly at Barry.

"I see that you, too, already know," he said, relieved. "Then, I'm not the only one bearing this heavy burden."

"I knew nothing," Barrison cut him short, drily.

"But... but you yourself brought up his sickness?" said the priest, at the edge of panic.

"I bluffed—and caught you," replied Barry, severely. He glanced out the window of the carriage. "We have only a few minutes left before we reach Tarford Manor, so you must enlighten me. And please, do not omit any detail."

Barry sat back in his seat, putting his crossed hands under his chin and staring into the eyes of the Man of the Cloth.

Father Howard thought for a brief moment, before beginning. He had sworn to never reveal what had been confided to him, but if Sir Henry's sanity depended on it, he had to break that promise. Besides, it hadn't been said in Confession, but during an informal conversation after Mass.

"It was last month, the fourth, if I remember correctly," he began. "The first Sunday of every month, I try to have a sermon that's a little more pragmatic than most, insisting on the benefits of generosity towards others rather than going into purely spiritual considerations. I have long come to the realization that it is good to alternate between the concrete and the abstract. That allows the faithful to see a connection between their own lives and religion."

Barry sighed with impatience. Father Howard cleared his throat.

"In brief," he continued, "it was during that sermon that I noticed for the first time Sir Henry's interest. I was enchanted by it. *After all these years,* I told myself, *I have succeeded in making him conscious of the truth of my words.* That was the reason that I hurried to join him after Mass—to tell him. So, I caught up with him, and saw immediately that his face was sad and gray. Something was wrong, obviously. That wasn't the Sir Henry I knew."

The priest interrupted himself. Barry had closed his eyes, but motioned to continue with his hand.

"I am not asleep, Father; I'm concentrating. Go on, please."

"We went down the steps and walked together for a while, side by side, in silence. A troubled silence, too. Then, I put my hand on his shoulder and made him look at me straight in the eyes. And he began to confide in me, admitting that he had an incurable disease, something he had caught in India, and that his days were numbered. He didn't want to tell me more, however, and made me promise to keep it a secret."

The Churchman bowed his head, visibly distressed.

"A promise that I have just broken..."

"For his benefit, Father," said Barry, who still had his eyes closed. "I thank you for that confession. I understand how difficult that must have been for you."

He opened his eyes.

"Ah! We're here!" he continued. "Obviously, all that was said between us shall remain confidential. I don't ask you to make me a promise, Father," he ended with a smile, "but just to trust me."

The carriage door opened. The driver had brought a large umbrella to shelter his passengers. Barry got out without waiting. Father Howard remained alone for a few seconds, as if overcome by his confession.

"Come on, Father!" said the detective, who was waiting patiently under the umbrella. "A good evening awaits us!" he added in a pleasant voice.

Man is decidedly a strange being, thought the priest.

He got out painfully from the carriage and the two men walked toward the door of Tarford Manor.

4.

Alfred opened the door right after Barry knocked. He stood to one side to let the two men enter and hurried to take their coats. He presented his respects to Father Howard, telling him that he was relieved to see him that evening.

"God bless you, Father," concluded the old butler with a preoccupied air.

"God bless you too, Alfred. Rest assured that you are of precious help to Sir Henry."

The butler smiled sadly. "I sometimes wonder about, Father..."

"What? Nothing happened?" asked Barry, frowning.

Alfred shook his head. "No, not that I know, Sir Barry, but Sir Henry has been strangely excited since earlier and the arrival of his first guests..."

"*Strangely excited*? What do you mean?"

"As I said. He's been very talkative, laughing a lot, and loudly too, as if he sought to hide serious concerns behind an apparent lack of care."

"Has he shared his motives with you?"

"No, not in the least."

"Have you noticed any other unusual details?"

"As for that, yes. Everything since yesterday afternoon has been strange. Sir Henry's other three guests are perfect strangers to me. Frankly, to see so many new faces in this old manor perturbs me."

Barry smiled in a way that he wanted to be comforting.

"There is nothing strange about that, Alfred. It's just your suspicious nature reasserting itself."

"Certainly, Sir, I can't deny it," replied the old butler, bowing slightly. "But Sir Henry shut himself up with that doctor for almost an hour, just after his arrival. And it was after that conversation that his behavior changed."

Barry approached Alfred. He could see the fatigue and sadness in the old servant's eyes.

"Alfred, would you please introduce us? Trust me, I shall take care of everything."

The old man returned his gaze, shining with held-back tears. He sighed, his shoulders sagging.

"Of course, Sir Barry. I have complete confidence in you, as you well know."

He started down the corridor, leading them to the main drawing room.

"If you gentlemen will please follow me..."

Alfred opened wide the doors and stood back to let the two men enter. The room had been prepared for the circumstance. A large table had been set up in front of the fireplace. The low table had been put away in a corner, as had the leather chairs. A new fire was already burning in the grate, and the wood box was filled with logs waiting their turn. Near the table, Sir Henry was talking to his guests, two men and a woman. The discussions stopped and the gazes converged on the new arrivals.

"My dear Barry!" exclaimed Sir Henry.

He rushed toward the duo who had just crossed the threshold and approached the detective. The two men greeted each other with a warm handshake. Then Sir Henry turned toward Father Howard, who had remained in the background. The master of the house gave him a big smile and motioned him to come forward.

"Lady and gentlemen," Sir Henry began, "allow me to introduce to you Sir Barry Barrison and Father Howard Fletcher, our local priest. That man of infinite goodness officiates at a church a few streets from here. He's one of the few men on Earth who knows almost all there is to know about me, even what should hardly be admitted."

He paused for a moment, lost in his memories. "I must be thankful for the secret of the confessional, without which my turpitudes would be revealed to all!"

Father Howard cleared his throat.

"Have no fear, Henry. You know very well that those exchanges remain strictly between you, Our Lord, and your priest."

Sir Henry put his hand on the priest's shoulder.

"Fortunately, Father, fortunately. But, please, come and meet my other guests. Barry and I will join you in a moment."

Father Howard did so and walked toward the table, introducing himself to each of the other guests in turn. Remaining with Barry, Sir Henry smiled at him.

"My friend, thank you for having answered my invitation," he said. "If you will allow me, I would like to introduce you personally to each person present here."

Barry consented with a nod of his head. Sir Henry motioned with his hand and Barry stepped toward the table. Father Howard, his mouth full, was already in the middle of a conversation with a man of stern appearance. He nodded his head regularly, while helping himself to varied canapés, answering his questioner, who, however, remained impassive.

Sir Henry led Barry to the far end of the table. There was sitting an old woman of advanced age, who wore a fancy hat decorated with cherries, little birds and lace ribbons. She was nibbling on a canapé that she had trouble chewing because of her failing teeth. She quickly lifted her astonished gaze at the approach of the two men and stared at them. Sir Henry greeted her with deference and turned toward his friend.

"Barry, allow me to introduce my friend, Countess Brunhild von Wachter, who has done me the immense pleasure of accepting my invitation for this evening. Countess, this is Sir Barry Barrison, one of my oldest friends."

The old woman nodded in Barry's direction without speaking,

"The Countess, in addition to being one of the most eminent ambassadors from that beautiful country that is

Austria, is also a famous medium. She has kindly agreed to hold a séance after dinner."

Bowing toward the old woman, he kissed her hand delicately, adding, "Thank you again, my very dear Countess, for having agreed to initiate Philistines like us into your mysterious Art."

"The pleasure is entirely mine, Sir Henry," responded the old lady, rolling her *r*s. "It is an honor to be invited to your beautiful manor."

Barry came forward and greeted the Countess. "If Sir Henry invited you tonight, it's because he has great respect for your skills. I can only be impatient to take part in this séance after dinner. What city are you from, if I may ask?"

"What a question, Sir Barry! From Vienna, of course!" She made a slightly gesture of annoyance with her hand. "Where else could I come from, do you think?"

"Pardon me, Countess, I should have guessed," replied Barry, with a polite smile on his face. He took on a dreamy expression. "How I love to take a walk along the banks of the Danube, most of all during the summer at sunset when the temperatures start dropping. It's a magic moment. I had the opportunity to be there in 1873 for a major chess tournament which saw a crushing victory by the German grandmaster, Wilhelm Steinitz, against one of my fellow countrymen, Joseph Henry Blackburn. I was just learning the game at that time, and I was astonished by his ability to see eight or ten moves ahead..."

He paused for a second. The Countess stared at him.

"But, that wasn't the most important," he continued. "I confess shamelessly that each evening, before returning to my rooms, I loved to take a long walk along the riverbank, taking advantage of the tranquility of the place while going over the most remarkable moves of the day."

The old woman who had been on the point of swallowing the remainder of her canapé, interrupted, her mouth open. She frowned. "Pardon?"

Barry repeated: "The Danube, it's a magical place, isn't it?"

The Countess seemed to understand.

"Ah! Yes, a magnificent river, very pleasant, in fact to walk along it. But you must excuse me, Mr. Barrinson, at my age, with my head, it's sometimes difficult to understand everything you say. English is not my native language, you see."

"You are excused, dear Countess!" Sir Henry said. "We will leave you to enjoy these appetizers and we will see each other at diner."

He gave her a polite bow. Barry did the same. The old woman could then finish her canapé in peace. He then took Barry by the arm and tried to draw him toward another guest. But Barry refused to move.

"Countess, it's Barrison, not Barrinson," he told the old woman, smiling.

"Come on, Barry, let her finish her *petit four* in peace," scolded Sir Henry.

"Sorry, Henry, but I don't like people to mispronounce my name," responded Barry with the same tone.

They then approached Father Howard, who was still engaged in a major conversation with the fortyish year-old man with a stern expression. His features reminded Barry of the statues on Easter Island. He had short graying hair, with a well-defined part on the left. His almond eyes looked at the priest with an odd intensity.

Sir Henry interrupted the conversation.

"Barry, allow me to introduce you to Doctor Phileas Longwood of Bristol. Doctor, this is Sir Barry Barrison."

The man turned away from the priest and faced Barry, greeting him with a quasi-military nod.

"This eminent practitioner had the courtesy of answering a long letter that I had sent him some weeks ago. I told him about my troubles and my concerns, and he was kind enough to travel all the way to London to have a conversation with me. "

Barry bowed stiffly in front of the doctor.

"I am delighted to make your acquaintance, Doctor. I'm glad to find out that Sir Henry requested your assistance, and I can't but assume that you will be of invaluable help to him. May I ask what your specialty is?"

Longwood put the little dish in which he had placed several hors d'oeuvres back on the table, and smiled at Barry.

"In my turn, Sir Barry," he began in an affable manner, "I am honored to meet the man whose praises Sir Henry has sung to me for such a long time. And, if I may say so," he continued, "I have the impression that you are the one who holds his head out of the water—not me."

Speaking to his host, he added: "Please excuse me for the analogy, Sir Henry."

Sir Henry smiled. "You are completely excused, Doctor. Your analogy is just." Then, looking slightly embarrassed, he added to Barry, "I didn't mention our epistolary relationship to you because I was afraid that it might bother you. I thought you might find it weak, or ridiculous of me to rely on someone unknown to me to try to understand what was happening to me, when I had only to ask you."

"Not at all," interrupted Barry. "First, the idea of doubting the competence of this gentleman never entered my mind. Also, I have total confidence in the soundness of your judgment, and only want you to take care of yourself as best as possible."

Father Howard coughed, reminding them that he was a part of the conversation.

"It certainly wouldn't be like Sir Barry to reproach you, Henry, for surrounding yourself with other professionals in whom you have confidence."

"Indeed," Barry confirmed. "I would never allow myself to do so. However," he continued, "I believe that the learned gentleman has not yet answered my question."

"'I am a psychiatrist," replied the Doctor with a smile that was not faked. "I listen to other people and, as any good practitioner, I react. If I believe what I am hearing right now, I deduct that, despite your words of reassurances, Sir Barry, you do find my presence rather inopportune. At least, the tone of your voice would appear to indicate so. Am I wrong?"

"I'm afraid in this instance, you are, Doctor. The tone of my voice only reflects the genuine concerns that I feel about my friend's troubled circumstances. That concern goes well beyond my ordinary prejudices."

"I share your concern, Sir Barry," replied the doctor. "Sir Henry has confessed some of his troubles to me."

"You see me delighted, Doctor," Barry replied. "I am happy that Sir Henry has confided in you, and that he told you about his troubles. What puzzles me is that he only spoke to me about them very recently. If I recall correctly, he said he contacted you several weeks ago, correct?"

"Yes," Longwood replied, "but I assure you, you do not realize what fulsome and easy words of praise your friend uses when he talks about you."

Sir Henry interrupted them.

"Gentlemen, come now, let's stay courteous, if you will, please. I have brought you this evening, one as well as the other, to be in the company of people I hold in high esteem. Don't spoil this by vain and prideful quarrels."

He looked with insistence at the two men, assuring himself that he had been understood. Seeing their silence, he continued:

"Come, Barry, I still have one more guest to introduce you to. Phileas, take full advantage of those hors d'oeuvres."

He smiled at the doctor before drawing Barry toward the last visitor, who was sitting calmly in one of the two armchairs usually placed in front of the fireplace, but which, exceptionally, had been set a little to the side. The man was sipping a glass of sherry, his eyes looking into the distance. Seeing Sir Henry in the company of Barry approaching, he rose to greet them. He bore a large, dark, perfectly trimmed moustache which ended in little concentric circles. Bald, plump, he was stuffed into a suit a little too tight for him, and a few drops of sweat looked like pearls on his forehead. He had a ruddy complexion and was short of breath.

"Barry, let me introduce you to Paul McLannish, my solicitor and the executor of my will, and a proud Scotsman as he likes it to be known. Paul, this is Sir Barry Barrison."

Barry held his hand out to McLannish. The two men exchanged a firm handshake.

"Delighted to make your acquaintance," the Scotsman began in a heavily accented voice. "I am late in making your acquaintance, Sir Barry. Sir Henry has been singing your praises to me for such a long time."

Barry hesitated an instant, then said, "How do you do Sir," with a brief nod of his head. "I am confused about the praise you mention. I promise you, in all modesty, that it must have been grossly exaggerated."

A short laugh from the other turned into a coughing fit. He pointed an index finger toward the detective.

"Ah, Sir Henry warned me that you would deny it. He knows you more than well!"

He began to laugh wholeheartedly and coughed some more. He rummaged around in the pocket of his jacket and put a handkerchief over his mouth. He made a gesture of excuse with his hand and stepped aside to calm his coughing fit.

"Your solicitor?" Barrison inquired, without taking his eyes off the little Scotsman. "What about Horace Abbeville?"

"Oh, he was getting on in years, and he confided to me several months ago that he felt very tired. He finally decided to close his practice, and I then decided to look for a new solicitor."

"And you had to go to Scotland? London wasn't filled with enough lawyers for your taste?"

Sir Henry raised an eyebrow.

"Ah! You noticed right away that he is a Scotsman? You always surprise me, Barry. However, you are wrong on one point."

"Which one?"

"He lives in London and has been for many years."

Barry took a handkerchief out of his pocket and wiped his hands.

"So be it," he answered.

The doors to the large drawing room opened. Alfred entered ringing a bell.

"Lady and Gentlemen, dinner is served."

He stood to one side, and bowed, inviting the six guests to enter the dining room.

5.

Alfred guided the guests toward the large dining room of Tarford Manor. They entered down a long, richly-decorated corridor. At regular intervals, there were paintings signed by Richard Doyle, John Alexander, and others, enhanced by their sumptuous frames and perfect lighting. Sir Henry was very proud of his private collection, so he stopped in front of an alcove where the greatest and most majestic of his paintings was enthroned— the portrait of a young, red-haired woman wearing a purple dress. She was standing in the door of a modest cottage, looking outside, her eyes gazing into the distance, holding a silk shawl tightly around her frail, pale shoulders.

"Here is what I consider the master piece of my modest collection," Sir Henry declared, with a note of pride. "This is *April Love* and is the work of Sir Arthur Hughes. He painted it in or around 1850."

The Countess came closer and put on her little glasses to better examine the details. McLannish stifled another coughing fit with his handkerchief. Barry remained at the back of the group, taking advantage of the moment to ask a question in Alfred's ear. The old butler shook his head negatively.

After everyone had had time to admire the portrait, Sir Henry resumed his walk. Alfred, who had gone ahead, waited respectfully for his master and his guests to arrive at the expensive wooden doors which led into the most imposing room of the manor. At a nod from Sir Henry, the old butler pushed open the doors. The immense double doors opened silently, and Alfred stepped back to let the guests enter. The dining room was grand and imposing. Located at the heart of Tarford Manor, it was the most remarkable room of all. Its ceiling was over four meters high. An enormous chandelier hung from it, held in place by four magnificent decorative chains. Several hundred candles, all lit, gave a soft glow to the décor. The immense table had been laid for the occasion. Two huge fireplaces, one on the east wall and another on the west wall, warmed the room with their robust fires. The guests couldn't hide their wonder. Father Howard, his mouth open, stood for several seconds on the threshold. He approached Barry, whose sharp eyes had reviewed every detail.

"I didn't even know the existence of this room. It's... splendid," he said with an intake of breath.

"It is that indeed."

The priest frowned. "I fear Sir Henry must have a serious announcement to make."

Barry raised an eyebrow. "Why do you say that, Father? Have you just noticed something strange in his behavior?"

"No, nothing at all, but I think that this room can only witness very important announcements. It is much too grand for a mere dinner among friends."

Barry smiled. "Don't you think that Sir Henry simply wants to gather his guests in a magnificent setting only to spend a most pleasant evening?"

Father Howard looked doubtful. "Perhaps. I hope so, in any case." He sighed deeply as if he wanted to magically erase his concerns, adding, "I hope that Alfred's food will be worthy of this setting."

"Rest reassured, Father. Alfred is a magician of the haute cuisine," said Sir Henry, who had caught these last words.

He invited them to come into the room and approach the perfectly set table.

"Take your places, please. Alfred!"

"Sir?"

"I am turning our guests over to you."

The butler bowed and excused himself. He gave Barry a long and knowing look and sat Father Howard to the left of Sir Henry. Barry, for his part, found himself facing his host, with the Countess to his right and Doctor Longwood to his left. McLannish sat to Sir Henry's right. The master of the house took his chair last. Alfred filled all of the glasses and left. Barry stood up suddenly.

"I know that this is not the tradition, Sir Henry, but will you permit me to speak before you do?"

"By all means, please, Barry" replied Sir Henry, standing up. "You are a much better speaker than I am. I must confess that I wasn't looking forward to making a speech. So, I gladly yield my place."

He sat down again, leaving Barry standing alone. The detective cleared his throat. All eyes were riveted on him.

"Lady and Gentlemen, rest assured that I won't be long. I think that you, like me, are anxious to taste the excellent dishes that Alfred has prepared for us. So, I will ask only a single question from our host..."

Sir Henry sat up straight in his chair.

"…Why do we merit the distinct honor of sitting in your dining room? I am almost certain that you have an important message to announce. Then, don't make us languish any longer; tell us now, so that we can eat in total serenity!"

He smiled at his friend and sat down again. There was silence in the room. Nothing was heard except for the crackling of the fire. After a few seconds, Sir Henry stood up, pushing back his seat in a ceremonial fashion. At that moment, the doors opened again. Alfred, unaware of the awkward silence, entered, pushing in front of him a large silver cart covered with platters overflowing with varied entrées, each one more appetizing than the next. He was preparing to serve the first course when he suddenly noticed the troubled silence that hung in the air, so he interrupted himself and stood still.

"My dear Barry," Sir Henry began, "learn first of all that I am honored to have you—all of you—here this evening; but you are mistaken. I have no announcement to make. I only wanted to use this a warm and friendly place for our dinner…" He then noticed Alfred, who was still waiting, stiff as a statue. "Furthermore," he hurried to conclude, "I see that my faithful butler is here, waiting to serve us." He motioned him to start. "I wish you a healthy appetite."

Relieved, Alfred began serving the dishes as Sir Henry sat again. The atmosphere relaxed as the first guests began tasting the food.

"You have surpassed yourself, Alfred!" said the nobleman.

"Thank you, Sir Henry," the butler replied. "I hoped that you would like it."

"I have no doubt about that."

"Has Sir chosen the wine?"

"Yes, Alfred. You will find the bottles labeled in the cupboard. You have only to bring them with each course."

"Very good, Sir."

The butler went to a little adjacent door, located next to the nearest fireplace.

Barry raised an eyebrow. "Is Alfred no longer minding the wine cellar?"

"Ordinarily, yes; but to occupy my mind, I have decided to sort out, count and label the bottles in my cellar. I thought that since I seem to be losing my mind, it would be a good way to exercise it."

"You are not losing your mind, Sir Henry," Doctor Longwood interrupted him. "As I have already told you, I think that you are instead repressing certain facts from your past, and that self-induced amnesia has had repercussions n your short-term memory. It's as simple as that, and also, I think that you should avoid alcoholic drinks."

"Nonsense!" replied Sir Henry. "It may be that simple for you, Doctor, but not for me. I would prefer to remember those buried facts in order to exorcise those memories and regain my memory again."

"It will take time, Sir Henry—and patience."

Alfred had returned and was now serving wine. When he finished, he stepped back and waited, standing by the fireplace.

"Perhaps a séance will help you, Sir Henry?" suggested the Countess.

"I'm counting on that very much, my dear Countess." Sir Henry replied. "It is my dearest wish."

Father Howard, who had remained silent until then, cleared his throat. "Excuse me, Sir Henry, and my apologies, Countess, if I appear to be impolite..."

The old woman shook her head.

"Do you really think that spiritualism is the correct response to a memory loss?" asked the Priest, who felt uncomfortable about such things.

Countess van Wachter answered, "Spiritualism must not be confused with black magic, Father. That is an old cliché. Spiritualism only allows the soul to be placed in a restful state, more relaxed than sleep, and therefore, the possibility of memories returning becomes easier."

"I understand. Sir Henry, have you already taken part in this type of séance?"

"Never, Father, I admit," replied their host. "But I don't think that it could be more painful than sitting in a Confessional, could it?"

He winked at the priest and chuckled. McLannish had another coughing fit, then sneezed. His face became red when he tried to control the assault from his chest.

"Excuse me," he said, after a short silence, "but I find Sir Henry's comment rather amusing. As for me," he continued in his pronounced accent, "I would be more afraid of going into a confessional than into a séance— even if ghosts were brought forth.

"You put that in your will," cut in Barry, putting down his glass of water.

The smile vanished from the solicitor's face. "I don't understand what you mean, Sir Barry?"

"Nothing really," replied the detective, with a polite smile. "It was just a small bit of humor. I apologize if I offended you. That was not what I intended, but, since we're talking about wills, I would like to know, Sir Henry, if you have recently changed yours?"

Sir Henry threw a look at McLannish, then replied. "Actually, yes, Barry. I really can't hide anything from you, can I? Alfred?"

The butler came forward. "Sir?"

"Take this course away and serve the next one. That was excellent."

"Yes," added the Countess. "Very good *foie gras*."

"Prepared with the greatest of care," added the old man.

"Your little salad was equally marvelous," added Longwood, while taking a look at his pocket watch.

"Thank you, Sir."

"And the wine was remarkable," added Father Howard.

"A French claret," cut in Sir Henry, "from the Bergerac region, to be accurate."

"I agree," added Barry, "a fine choice, Sir Henry, but a red would have been an even better one."

Sir Henry, seemed surprised.

"Surely, my friend, you must know that *foie gras* is best enjoyed with a white wine."

"Pardon me, Sir Henry. I am not a gourmet like you are."

Sir Henry smiled back. "You are totally excused. For once, I am the one who's corrected you."

Barry smiled contritely. Alfred left the room after having cleared the table. Now certain that the butler had closed the door, Sir Henry continued, his face somber.

"I did change my will, Barry. That's the reason for Mr. McLannish presence here."

"What does that have to do with Alfred?"

"I beg your pardon?"

"You were careful to wait until Alfred had left the room before confiding your new dispositions. I then deducted that there is some rapport with him. Am I wrong?"

Sir Henry hesitated and rubbed his chest with his left hand. He grinned a little before continuing.

"No, you are not wrong. And since we are sharing confidences, I have also included Farther Howard in my will."

The octogenarian almost choked while drinking his Bergerac. He put his glass back on the table, trembling and coughing.

"Me? But you know that's impossible."

Sir Henry smiled.

"I expressed myself badly, Father. It isn't you that I included in my will, but your parish."

"I still don't understand."

"It's very simple, Father. When Barry suggested that I should invite you tonight, I reminisced over all those years of catechism and secret confessions. You have shaped my youth and my life," he said with emphasis. "It was then unthinkable that I should not thank you in one way or another."

Speechless, the priest stared at Sir Henry.

"However, Father, I must ask you for a favor."

"What?" asked the priest, confused.

"That of being my executor and seeing that all the terms of my will are carried out to the letter. I do not want it to be invalidated and have your parish deprived of the small legacy that I have left it."

"Sir Henry," interrupted McLannish, "this is neither the place nor the time."

The host turned slightly purple.

"My word! You are right. It must be that fine wine that made me lose my train of thought," he added with a smile.

Once more the doors opened. Alfred entered, preceded by the scent of a piece of meat delicately cooked. He hesitated, waiting for that sign of approval to approach. It wasn't long in coming.

"Come, Alfred, serve us! The smell coming from that roast inflames our appetite. Don't make us wait!"

Sir Henry once again rubbed his chest. Father Howard looked at Barry. The detective read total disbelief in his eyes.

The butler served each of the guests and went to get a new bottle of wine. Longwood was arranging his watch in his vest pocket when he interrupted his gesture.

"Countess? Is there a problem?"

The old woman had become totally white and was staring at an invisible point above Sir Henry's head.

"*Geist! Geist!*[2]" she murmured, trembling.

"What is she saying?" Sir Henry began.

He made a gesture as if to push back his chair, stopped for an instant, then fell forward. His head struck his plate, which broke under the impact.

Alfred dropped the bottle of wine he was holding. It broke into a thousand pieces when it hit the floor. Doctor Longwood jumped up quickly, rushing to examine Sir Henry. McLannis had another coughing fit, stronger than all the others. He was choking. Barry Barrison had pushed back his chair and had gone around the table to help the doctor take care of his friend. Father Howard, panicked and confused, went to help the old woman, but she had fainted. The priest had just enough time to catch her before she collapsed in her chair. Longwood placed two fingers on Sir Henry's neck.

"He's dead," he said in a colorless voice.

---

[2] Ghost!

6.

The Countess had been stretched out on one of the couches in the drawing room. A wet cloth lay her fore-head; she had recovered consciousness, but remained speechless. McLannish was sitting on a chair beside her, holding her hand. The solicitor was staring into the distance and seemed lost in his thoughts. Standing near the fireplace, his arms crossed on his chest, Barry Barrison smoked his pipe mechanically. His eyes were fixed on the hypnotic flames dancing in the hearth. At the other end of the room, Alfred had collapsed in an armchair facing the window. The old butler had not said a single word since Sir Henry had fallen face down onto his plate an hour earlier. He wept silently from time to time.

The door opened and Dr. Longwood entered, accompanied by Father Howard and Dr. Samuel Witherden. Barry had gone to fetch a medical doctor he knew right after Sir Henry's collapse, returning a half hour later in a carriage with him. Longwood went over to the old butler to try to comfort him. The priest went toward Barry, his face overwhelmed, accompanied by the newcomer.

"What tragedy," Father Howard began.

Dr. Witherden shook Barry's hand, trying to make his handshake as comforting as possible.

"His heart?" Barry asked simply.

"Yes, unfortunately, there is no doubt—it was a massive heart attack. I suppose the stress of the last few days, his lack of sleep, his fear of insanity, and the alcohol drank this evening, were too much for his heart."

"Did you know that Sir Henry had a weak heart, Barry?" asked Father Howard.

"No," replied the detective. "He never mentioned anything about that to me."

"Perhaps he didn't know anything about it himself?"

"It is possible."

"What are we going to do, Barry?"

"There is nothing more that can be done tonight, Father, except take leave of these people and return tomorrow to help with the necessary formalities."

Perplexed, Father Howard looked at Barry. He was about to reply when Dr. Witherden put his hand on his shoulder. The priest stopped. With a glassy stare, Barry crossed the room and approached Alfred. He said a few words to Longwood, who left both of them alone. Barry knelt down beside the old man and murmured to him. The butler acquiesced, sitting upright slowly. Barry then returned to the center of the room, holding out a hand to McLannish, who had risen.

"We can go ahead with the reading of the will tomorrow, if that is convenient for you," he said in a neutral voice.

"That will be perfect," answered the solicitor. "Shall we say, ten o'clock?"

"Very good. Ten o'clock it is." Barrison bowed. "Father, I believe we can go now."

Dumbfounded, Father Howard just mumbled and mechanically followed Barry. Doctor Witherden joined them. Alfred insisted on accompanying them to the door, despite the detective's protests.

The little group left in the grand drawing room stood in silence. A handful of minutes, which seemed like an eternity, passed before Dr. Longwood approached the Countess.

Suddenly, there was a knock on the door. Barry Barrison entered. Behind him was Father Howard, looking dumbfounded, and Doctor Witherden.

7.

"Did you forget something?" asked McLannish, coughing again.

"Ah, your coughing fits have started again! Astonishing! However, since Sir Henry's death, you have been very calm. Is something bothering you?"

"I beg your pardon?" the other man answered, frowning.

A fourth man entered the room. Wearing a dark suit, a gray overcoat with a large collar, and a melon-colored hat, he was proudly wearing a large mustache clipped according to the current fashion.

"Please excuse me for my impertinence," Barry continued with emphasis. "May I introduce you to Chief Inspector Harvey Lipperstein of Scotland Yard. He is here at my request."

The Countess moved about on her couch.

"Who is he?" she murmured.

"Merely a friend, Countess."

Father Howard collapsed, more than he sat down, in his chair. He seemed totally lost. Alfred had also returned to the drawing room. All sadness had disappeared from his face. No longer could one see anything on his expression except hatred and anger.

"Could we know what is the meaning of all this?" asked Phileas Longwood, moving toward Barry.

"Certainly, Doctor. Chief Inspector Lipperstein is here to arrest you for attempted murder of Sir Henry Tarford."

"What! That's shameful!" exclaimed Longwood, furious.

Lipperstein advanced and interposed himself between Barry and the Doctor. McLannish had another violent coughing spell.

"Lady, Gentlemen, please be calm, I beg you," said the policeman. Then, turning toward Alfred, he continued, "Would you be kind enough to get my men who are waiting outside?"

"With pleasure," the butler answered.

He left the room and returned a few minutes later accompanied by several uniformed policemen who advanced toward McLannish, Countess von Wachter, and Doctor Longwood. The police surrounded them and took them outside.

"Don't forget the dead man," Barry added.

"Don't worry, Sir Barry," cut in Lipperstein. "They won't forget him."

Calm returned to the drawing room. Barry Barrison returned to the fireplace and cleaned out his pipe.

"Are you finally going to explain to me what happened, Barry? I am lost," asked Father Howard.

The amateur sleuth turned around, a big smile on his face. "I can understand why you are, Father. I almost got lost, myself—and all because of you!" He pointed an accusing finger at the old man. Then he burst out laughing. "But rest reassured, Father, you didn't know anything about it."

"I don't know anything now."

Barry sat down on one of the couches, crossed his legs, and let out a puff of white smoke from his pipe.

"Everything seemed simple to me at first, even if what Sir Henry described in his letter mystified me a little. My suspicions began during my visit yesterday. I saw a very perturbed Sir Henry, who seemed detached from himself. Then he made a clumsy mistake during his ninth move! What a monumental blunder!"

Father Howard shook his head. "Pardon? I'm already not following you."

"When going into the drawing room, I found my friend deep into a game of chess, something which both of us play during each of my visits, or even by post."

"That I know, but I still don't understand."

"You do remember that Sir Henry and I met each other during a chess competition several years ago. And we always began our play using an opening called *the Quiet Game*—it's a classic opening, not very aggressive, but one that fits our mood. So, you see, to watch him making such a mistake during his ninth move was unthinkable."

"Distraction? Forgetfulness? A lapse in memory? Sir Henry said in his letter that he did experience some."

"No, that would be inconceivable!" Barry hammered in a strong voice. "It'd be like forgetting how to walk at twenty. I couldn't accept it. The only possibility was that my host was not Sir Henry!"

The sentence resounded like the crack of a whip.

"What? How could it not be Sir Henry?" stammered Alfred.

"And yet, that man was not Sir Henry; I'm certain of it," Barrison repeated, smiling.

"Then who was it?" continued the old butler, as lost and haggard as the priest.

"His twin brother Philip Tarford."

"Oh! My God! How is that even possible? I didn't know Sir Henry had a brother…"

"Yes, my dear Alfred. Presumed lost or dead in Africa when they were both young men. I had all but forgotten about him. But I had my first doubt during our conversation in the vestibule. Do you remember? The tea..."

"Yes, I remember, but I don't see..."

"Think back," Barry continued. "Let's suppose that Philip had returned to England to take revenge on his brother, who had enjoyed all the wealth of the Tarford family for almost fifty years, while he lived in filth somewhere on the Dark Continent. He had the idea to usurp his brother's identity, make him disappear, and enjoy the family's fortune. He began to hang around Tarford Manor, observing Sir Henry, picking up all his habits, and his way of life. He copied his appearance and his way of dressing. Then, he tested their resemblance, and what better way of doing that than facing a man who had known Sir Henry all his life?"

He paused. Father Howard and Alfred were listening, open-mouthed. Satisfied, Barry continued.

"To meet Father Howard, the family priest, face to face! It was Philip, I'm sure, not Henry, that you saw that fateful Sunday when he confided his incurable illness to you. He had succeeded in getting the real Sir Henry away from London that day in a manner that we will no doubt discover later, and had taken his place. He had to test you—you were the first step in his plan! And it worked perfectly, because you didn't notice the switch, and were quick to tell me about that pretended illness when I came to pick you up!"

"So that's why, when I wanted to follow up on our conversation the week after, he told me he had no idea of what I was talking about and denied having any incurable illness?"

"Exactly!" Barry confirmed. "And it served a further purpose that was an integral part of Philip's plan: to make Sir Henry doubt his own sanity!"

Barry relit his pipe.

"That also explains the so called *forgetfulness* of Sir Henry about his walks in the neighborhood. Copying his actions and gestures, Philip passed himself off as his brother on the days Sir Henry had decided to stay home at the Manor. The witnesses to whom I spoke left me with no doubt: we were in the presence of two men with identical appearances, but different behavior. In fact, that was his first mistake. He did not anticipate that those who crossed his brother's path every day would still notice a slight difference in their behavior. But let's return to the matter of the tea, my dear Alfred…"

Barry stood up, went to get a large glass of water, then returned and sat down. He placed the glass in front of him after having drunk a large swallow.

"Philip had gotten wind of the letter that Sir Henry had sent to me," he continued. "So he had to act quickly. He decided to contact his brother in order to arrange a direct confrontation between them. That took place the day before yesterday, when Henry asked you to go purchase some tea for him."

"Philip, you mean?" asked Father Howard, who still didn't understand.

"No, it was really Sir Henry who asked Alfred to go and buy some tea. Undoubtedly, he thought that he would succeed in controlling his brother. The conversation that you overheard, Alfred, was not the ramblings of a sick man talking to himself, but an argument between the two brothers. As for the noise you then heard, it was likely the body of Sir Henry falling on the floor after his brother had struck him. His body was then hidden behind a large bureau by the time you returned with the tea."

"But, then, where is the real Sir Henry?"

"I will come back to that in an instant, Father. But rest assured, Sir Henry is all right. All the pieces of the puzzle now come together perfectly. A twin who was supposed to be dead returns to take his brother's place. He dupes the family priest, manages to get into Tarford Manor, thanks to Sir Henry's weakness, and takes his place without their faithful butler noticing anything. The trap is set—but for whom?"

Barry put down his empty pipe on the table and continued:

"For me, obviously! Philip knew of the ties that bound Sir Henry and I. I was the only real obstacle to the success of his plan. It was necessary for him to convince me of the legitimacy of Sir Henry's death so that he could later claim his inheritance safely. However, I threw a figurative grain of sand into his careful scheme: I invited Father Howard! I noticed right away how the fake Sir Henry was perturbed by my suggestion, but he couldn't refuse and so, he had to invent something…"

Barrison paused.

"I must say that he improvised very well. That supposed change in his will that included you was ingenious. He knew how much your parish needs money, and thus, he hoped to lessen your doubts... if you had any…"

The priest shook his head. "No, I never had any doubt about Sir Henry. I was totally convinced, even being seated at his side. I was a little perturbed by the announcement concerning his will, but I took it as a further gesture of kindness."

"Well, Philip is anything but kind!" replied Barrison, tapping the palm of his hand on the arm of his chair. "He had long plotted his revenge. Nothing was going to thwart him. The ease with which he included you in his scheme just shows how intelligent and determined he was... just like his brother."

Barry picked up his tobacco pouch that he had left on the table. He stood up and went looking for an ashtray on the mantelpiece of the fireplace.

"I was suspicious of him when I left, but I still needed to confirm my suspicions before having him arrested. I wracked my mind a good part of the night wondering about these new friends of Sir Henry. Were they accomplices or innocent witnesses of Philip's crime."

He returned to sit down and emptied his pipe.

"The first person that the fake Sir Henry introduced me to was the Countess, an odd bird, to say the least, with a pronounced accent. Eccentric. Too much so? I didn't know. I then laid a trap for her..."

"What trap?" asked Lipperstein, standing, leaning against the fireplace.

Barry took his time lighting the bowl of his pipe before replying:

"She claimed to be Austrian, but when I said that Steinitz was German, she did not react. Now, all native Austrians would have known that the extraordinary Wilhelm Steinitz is Austrian, not German."

"Why did Philip want to have a false Austrian Countess among his guests?" asked Lipperstein, frowning.

Barry exhaled several clouds of white smoke before answering:

"That was a point that bothered me right to the end, my dear Lipperstein. As a matter of fact, I was going to ask you about it, but then, I figured it out. But before I answer your question, let me continue with what really happened this evening..."

Meanwhile, Alfred had calmed down. The poor man had gone from the deepest sadness to the most violent rage in a matter of hours. Now, he simply felt fatigued and exhausted. He was content to listen to Barry's explanations, happy that the real Sir Henry was safe; that was all that was important to him.

"Dr. Longwood was an interesting person, too. I am convinced that the man is actually knowledgeable about medicine, but likely more chemistry than psychology. When you search him, Harvey, I am sure that you will find a little flask of odorless and colorless liquid in his pocket."

"And what will that be?"

"Digitalis, my friend! Longwood made Philip drink some during their private interview that afternoon. Normally, digitalis is a strong poison, but diluted, prepared with care and taken in the right amount, it will only simulate a cardiac arrest. I was wondering why the good doctor was looking at his watch so regularly. He was calculating the time when the fake heart attack would occur, and he had to signal to the Countess. However, be careful! The flask you will find on him will not be a diluted solution. It was meant for the real Sir Henry, in order to kill him. Digitalis leaves no trace. It would have been impossible to determine if Sir Henry had been poisoned."

Alfred got up from his seat and came to sit down near Barry, asking: "You said that Sir Henry is alive, but where was he during the dinner?"

Barry smiled at the old man and replied, "How long have you not had access to the wine cellar?"

"For about a day, but why?"

"That's where Philip had locked up Sir Henry. Lipperstein's men found him there a short while ago, tired but in good health. That's why Philip didn't want you to go down in that cellar and why he had prepared the wine himself. That was his second mistake."

"Sir?"

"The Bergerac and the *foie gras*. Sir Henry would have known perfectly well that a white wine—especially a Bergerac—would not go well with *foie gras*, something Philip obviously didn't know. That definitely convinced me that we were not dealing with the real Sir Henry. But he made a third mistake…"

"A third?" Father Howard observed. "Trying to follow your reasoning makes me dizzy, Barry…"

Barrison chuckled. "I understand, Father, but his third mistake was the biggest and yet the one least likely to be noticed. And it was you who made me aware of it: the dining room."

"I don't understand," said Lipperstein. "Why not use that magnificent room to entertain one's guests?"

Alfred cleared his throat. "If I may be allowed, Sir Barry?"

"By all means, Alfred."

The old butler turned to face the man from Scotland Yard.

"In the Tarford family, the dining room is traditionally not used, except in unusual circumstances. Sir Henry remembered all those meals during which sad news were announced. That was the reason he never used it. He remembered those sad moments."

"In fact," Barry continued, "since I have known him, I have never been invited but for one time into that room, and that was in sad circumstance, too."

"The death of Miss Elizabeth," Alfred sighed.

Barry acquiesced.

"That was why after we were seated around the table, I asked the fake Sir Henry if he had a very particular reason for making us sit in that particular room. The response he gave only confirmed my opinion that he was an impostor."

Barry stood up.

"The rest is only details. McLannish must be a real solicitor. After all, someone like him was needed to rewrite the will, but in my opinion, he was much too nervous to be innocent. He never stopped coughing and his hands were constantly damp. I realized that when I shook hands with him.

"As for the Countess, she was Philip's back-up plan, in case the digitalis was too diluted to fake a real heart attack, or if he changed his mind at the last moment. I suppose, he would have faked seeing ghosts and sinking further into madness. In the presence of a priest, the likely diagnosis would have been even more credible..."

"But in that case," Lipperstein cut in, "Sir Henry wouldn't have been dead?"

"Yes, you are right, but I think you will find in McLannish's briefcase *two* different wills: one in case of death, and the other in case of mental incapacity."

There was silence. Alfred came and shook Barry's hand, saying:

"From the bottom of my heart, thank you, Sir Barry. You have given me back my master and that is the most beautiful gift you could have ever given me."

Barry smiled. "You're very welcome," was all he said. Then he gave him a comforting tap on the shoulder and added, "Sir Henry will be back the day after tomorrow. I am counting on you to take good care of him and say hello for me. I will drop by to see him in two days."

Alfred bowed.

"Father, will you accompany me?" asked Barry. "I have a carriage waiting."

The priest nodded, still dumbfounded by the amateur detective's revelations. Lipperstein had already left. Alfred had accompanied him to the door.

Left alone, Barry Barrison looked around the room. Noticing the chessboard in a corner, he went over to it, thought for a minute, then made his move. With a little satisfied smile, he then left the room, closing the door silently behind him.

Death Becomes Him

1.

The shimmering, soft morning light filled the office located on the fifth floor of a majestic London building on the Victoria Embankment. Busy flipping through the latest edition of the *Daily Telegraph,* Chief Inspector Harvey Lipperstein was riveted by the newspaper. It was late April 1900, and the news were, for the most part, about the International Exposition taking place in Paris.[3] Since its opening, two weeks earlier, that giant fair provoked the craziest reactions. There were articles about it every day.

Lipperstein put the paper back on his desk, stood up after picking up his still smoking cup of tea, and went to stand in front of the widow. His gaze rested on Waterloo Bridge, struck as always by its magnificence. Its gigantic arches plunged into the River Thames at regular intervals like the feet of a majestic stone giant. The reflections of the sun in the river made its waters sparkle, surrounding the limbs of the colossal project in a protective and kindly aura. Sipping some tear, the Chief Inspector's gaze went a little further—to the majestic dome of Saint Paul's Cathedral. Built over the ruins of the previous edifice, which had been destroyed in the Great Fire of

---

[3] The *Exposition Universelle* of 1900 was a world's fair held in Paris from 14 April to 12 November 1900 to celebrate the achievements of the century. It was visited by nearly 50 million, and displayed many technological innovations.

1666, it dominated, by its beauty, the skyline of the English capital.

Lipperstein sighed happily. He was proud of his city and its history. He returned to his desk, putting down his cup with caution. The last few years had been rather kind to him, with one near exception. He had started to lose his hair! If it had not been for that, it would have been difficult for anyone to guess that the Chief Inspector was nearing sixty. Tall, svelte, athletic, and always dressed tastefully, Lipperstein presented himself well.

His moustache was now a little less dark than when he had first joined the Yard, thirty years ago, but remained always perfectly trimmed. He used the time it took to think, emptying his head, concentrating on the scissors and the little comb. Every useless thought left him and he could concentrate on his open cases. He knew he didn't have the deductive powers of the many consulting detectives who lived in London, and with whom he worked occasionally on the toughest cases, but more than once, he had succeeded in solving a case that seemed to be hopeless.

That ritual was a recurring subject of discussions on the fifth floor among the men whom the Chief Inspector called his team. There were only a handful of policemen working under him. The Yard had not yet seen fit to hire more, and several offices were still empty. The Chief Inspector didn't enjoy being a "guv;" he liked to encourage the members of his team to work together and to forget about rank and status. Yes, he was Chief Inspector, but he didn't derive any glory from that title. For him, titles meant nothing; only results were important. And Lipperstein and his men succeeded more often than many of Scotland Yard's other detectives.

The Chief Inspector took a cigarette out of a pack of *Sportsman* sitting on top of a pile of files on his desk and lit it. He inhaled the first puff, held his breath for several seconds to enjoy it, before exhaling. The smoke floated around him in an ephemeral plume. There was a knock on the door.

"Come in!"

A young man of about thirty entered.

"What is it, Eddings?" asked the Chief Inspector, smiling at his subordinate. "And what are you doing here on a Sunday? Why aren't you at home with your family?"

"I was just passing," answered Eddings in a hoarse voice.

The Chief Inspector greeted him with a warm handshake, then returned to the little table on which he had placed the tea kettle.

"It's still warm; I made it when I arrived. Would you like a cup?"

Answering his own question, Lipperstein poured a cup of the still-steaming liquid.

"Tell me what you think of it. It's a new brand that I recently discovered. It's got a slight taste of ginger with a strong bouquet of jasmine. Since I have tasted it, I confess that I've become addicted to it. It's impossible not to drink several cups in the morning; if not, I catch a headache. You take sugar, don't you?" he continued, without turning around.

Smiling, he held the cup out to Eddings, then noticed the expression on the young man's face. Frowning, he returned to his desk and put the cup down while motioning to Eddings to sit down.

"Sit, sit. What's wrong?" Lipperstein asked, as he, too, sat down.

Eddings sat in the chair across the desk. His hands were trembling.

"You have to come to the *Queen's Pawn* at once, Guv."

After a silence, Lipperstein burst out laughing.

"What happened? Have you broken one of your drinking partners' nose again?"

Eddings was known in the team as having a short temper. He had been reprimanded more than once for his all too frequent fights when he was a little drunk, and he was on the verge of being sacked when Lipperstein had recruited him for his team. The Chief Inspector was a good judge of characters, and, despite his feisty personality, Eddings was a good and reliable officer. Up until now, the young man had never disappointed him.

"No, Guv, it's not that at all, but I would prefer if you... you..." the young man stopped; he had trouble controlling his voice.

"What is it then?"

"It's your friend, Guv."

"My friend? Which friend?"

"That amateur detective who works with us from time to time—Sir Barry Barrison."

"Yes, what about him? What happened to him?"

"He's dead, Guv!"

2.

The *Queen's Pawn* wasn't perhaps host to the most fashionable chess club in London, but it certainly was the oldest and the one with the best reputation. Founded in 1732, it was located off Guilford Street in a little dead end alley, well sheltered from the noises of the City. Since its opening, the number of people visiting it had only increased. What drew people to the *Queen's Pawn* was its friendly atmosphere and impeccable service; all players, no matter their ranks, were welcome. As the years went by, the more famous players joined, preferring its simplicity to other, more fashionable circles. Some even said that Siegbert Tarrasch[4] himself had come there incognito to play more than once against the English elite.

Situated in the middle of a magnificent rectangular garden, surrounded by an attractive wrought iron fence, the building had three stories. A broad stone walkway led to the main entrance. There, guests were greeted by several employees in livery, whose only occupation was to see to their well-being.

The ground floor served only one function. In addition to the entrance hall and the cloakroom, it featured an immense drawing room with an elaborately decorated high ceiling. Several straight chairs and comfortable armchairs were arranged around in the room around little tables, allowing guests to get together in small groups. More intimate spaces were also provided near the windows, giving the guests who chose to sit there more intimacy. Along the walls, several fire places put out soft, comforting warmth all day long.

The first floor was divided into several smaller sitting rooms where guests could relax after or before a game, order drinks, food, smoke, or read one of the many valuable books borrowed from the many bookshelves. All the rooms were built with the same design: rectangular, with one double window looking out to the

---

[4] (1862-1934) German grandmaster, widely considered to have been among the strongest chess players and most influential chess teachers of the late 19th and early 20th century.

garden. Their furnishings were also exactly identical. In addition to the chessboards, the clock and two seats, there was a low table and two additional chairs, generally placed in front of a little fireplace located along the wall facing the door. When the guests were still playing late at night, a big chandelier attached to the ceiling allowed them to continue without being concerned about light. There were thirty-two of these rooms, and they had been nicknamed the *white boxes* by the members.

The third and last floor was reserved for tournaments and charitable exhibits. It was a magnificent room. The beams crossed each other, forming a spider's web that seemed to cover all of the space. During one exhibit two years prior, more than a hundred and fifty people had played there simultaneously under the best tournament conditions. The rest of the time, that floor was reserved to general club assemblies, which occurred at least once each quarter

Driving one of the ten Panhard & Levassor automobiles purchased by Scotland Yard a few years earlier, Chief Inspector Lipperstein turned in his head the improbable news Eddings had given him less than an hour before: Barry Barrison was dead.

The young policeman hadn't been able to find out the exact circumstances of the amateur sleuth's death. He had left the Queen's Pawn in a hurry to report to his superior. He had just taken the time to call a doctor and to forbid access to the room where the dead man lay, until the police arrived.

Eddings knew that Barrison and Lipperstein were old friends, so he had rushed back to Scotland Yard. Despite the fact that his superior would be devastated by the news, he had no doubt that Lipperstein would want to be first on the scene.

He's dead, Guv.

That sentence still reverberated in Lipperstein's head, making him feel dizzy and clouding his vision. The Chief Inspector made a sharp turn to avoid hitting a careless pedestrian. He hardly heard the man's curses. He was lost in his thoughts and overcome with sorrow. He tried to remember if there had been any clues... As far as he knew, Barrison was not sick. He knew the man was discreet about his private life and rarely confided details of it; he was talkative only about his cases, but he wasn't aware of any investigation that might have caused his friend to be killed.

Lipperstein had spent more than one evening dining at Tarford Manor, where Barry had chosen to reside after Sir Henry's death a few years earlier, waiting for the legitimate heir—a distant American cousin—to grow up and take possession. Their relationship, which had been purely professional at first, had slowly grown into a very sincere friendship, tinged with mutual respect. He shook his head. *No, that's impossible. If Barry was in danger, I would have known about it.* He had bombarded Eddings with questions, but the young man hadn't known anything else.

Lipperstein parked his car right in front of the entrance of the *Queen's Pawn*. Several uniformed policemen were already there, preventing people from entering the building. He also spotted a group of people standing in front of the entrance, all talking in a very excited manner. There were five gentlemen speaking together, and another older man, alone, seated a little further off, on the steps, staring in the distance.

After stepping out of the car, Lipperstein produced his Scotland Yard identification and was allowed inside. Despite the generous rays of light still available, the Chief Inspector shivered. As he stepped in front of the group that was talking, the men stopped and looked at him with surprise. Lipperstein went into the reception area and looked around. A man of about sixty, with a sad expression and tearful eyes, came to meet him.

"I am sorry, Sir, but you can't come in..."

"I'm Chief Inspector Lipperstein of Scotland Yard," interrupted the detective. "Are you the owner?"

The man looked surprised, then he cleared his throat before answering:

"Er, yes, Chief Inspector. I'm William Featherstone, at your service."

He held out his hand to Lipperstein.

"Mister Featherstone, I'd like for you to take me to the dead man," Lipperstein answered, mechanically shaking the other man's hand.

"Of course, Chief Inspector. If you will follow me..."

Without waiting for confirmation, the publican led Lipperstein up the stairs to the first floor. The Chief Inspector followed him.

"We received instruction from Inspector Eddings not to let anyone in the room where Sir Barry's body was found—not even a doctor who's a member the club, Sir Geoffrey Hilldale."

"You acted correctly."

"I hope you will find who did that loathsome deed quickly," continued Featherstone, shaking his head. "Sir Barry was very popular here. What a tragedy!"

Lipperstein stood rooted to the spot. The other man turned around after a minute, surprised at no longer being followed.

"Something wrong, Chief Inspector?"

The detective stared at Featherstone, and asked:

"What do you mean, *who did that loathsome deed*?"

Featherstone hesitated for a moment then came back down the three steps that separated him from the policeman.

"I'm not sure I understand your question, Chief Inspector. Hasn't your man Eddings told you?"

"Told me what?" bellowed Lipperstein. "So Barry was murdered—is that what you're saying?"

Featherstone's silence was eloquent.

"Let's go. I must see this," said Lipperstein, his words cracking like the sound of a whip.

Featherstone made a half-turn, and started back up the stairs. They soon reached the landing. The publican went down a long corridor. They turned left twice. Lipperstein noticed at once the presence of two uniformed policemen standing guard before an opened door. He walked past his host, who had stepped aside to let him pass, and the two policemen, showing them his id, and entered the room.

Judging from the pieces of wood scattered near his feet on the floor, it had been broken into. He glanced around the room: it was small and private, just like all the others. There was a window on the left wall. Light flooded in, producing warmth. The chessboard was in its regular place, near the window. The pieces were in place, waiting for the first move. Against the wall, facing the door, was the small fireplace, with no fire in the grate. In front of it were two comfortable armchairs with high backs. The one on the right was empty; the one on the left was turned toward the hearth, preventing Lipperstein from seeing its occupant. Between the two was a little round table on which rested a cup of water, two glasses, an ashtray and a key.

Lipperstein stepped forward. He saw the top of a head, its brown hair perfectly combed. He hesitated. He was afraid of what he was going to see next. He took a deep breath then moved to stand in front of the armchair. Featherstone, who had remained at the door, saw him turn pale.

Barry Barrison was seated there. As always, he was dressed in a perfectly fitted suit—dark gray. His legs were crossed and his hands rested on the arms of the chair. His right hand was closed on his faithful pipe. His eyes were closed and the expression on his face breathed calm and tranquility. He seemed to be plunged in deep thought. There was a white handkerchief jutting out of his breast pocket. Just below it, a thin dagger was planted in his chest, right up to its guard. A small rivulet of blood had escaped from the wound and created a large dark brown stain over his chest.

3.

The Chief Inspector was now seated behind one of the tables in an adjacent room, recovering from the shock that the sight of his dead friend had caused. Meanwhile, young Eddings was trying to find potential witnesses.

Lipperstein had quickly regained control of himself. Whatever the pain that the ghastly sight had caused him, he had to treat the murder as any other case, and concentrate on seeking the truth. Someone had murdered his friend, and he would not rest until he (or she?) had been apprehended.

Featherstone was seated in front of him. The expression on the face of the fifty-year-old publican was one of anxiety. Clearly, he could never have imagined that such a thing could happen in his establishment. He constantly combed his salt and pepper hair with his hand, and cleared his throat at regular intervals. He was waiting for the Chief Inspector to speak, forcing himself to remain calm.

Finally, Lipperstein put down the small pencil with which he had been writing in his little notebook, smoothed his mustache and gave Featherstone a compassionate look.

"Mister Featherstone, this interview is going to be just as painful for you as it is for me," he began in a polite but firm tone. "Please, be as precise as you can in the answers to the questions I'm going to ask you."

Featherstone acquiesced silently after a new clearing of the throat.

"All right, let's start with the facts, such as you know them."

"Where do you want me to begin?"

"Well, can you tell me the time when Sir Barry arrived here?"

Featherstone pulled his chair forward and put his hands flat on the table in front of him.

"You must understand, Chief Inspector, that I am not constantly in the entrance hall watching the comings and goings of our patrons. Administrative tasks command a great deal of my time. Also, everyone moves a lot about—this is a pub and a chess club, not a prison."

"Understood, Mister Featherstone, but that wasn't my question."

They were interrupted by the door opening behind them. Eddings entered. Lipperstein turned toward him.

"Any news?" he asked.

"Doctor Hilldale has finished his preliminary examination. And I have carefully searched the room." He paused, looking perplexed, scratching his growing beard.

"And?" asked Lipperstein, impatiently.

"Well, there are certain details that I can't quite figure out."

"I'll get to this in a short while. We'll both examine the, er, crime scene." He had stopped for a brief moment, as if he was reluctant to use the word *crime*.

Eddings agreed silently and left, closing the door behind him. Lipperstein returned to his witness.

"If I understand correctly," he continued, "you're telling me that you have no idea when Sir Barry arrived?"

"I would say, about eight thirty, like every Sunday, but that's only a supposition on my part. He is—pardon me, was—a man of habits. He spent almost all of his Sundays here. Eight-thirty was his usual time."

Lipperstein looked at his watch. It was eleven fifty-three. He scribbled some notes.

"All right, then what happened?"

"I checked the first floor about twenty minutes later. Sir Barry was sitting in the room where he was found, playing a game with Arthur Fell, one of our usual guests. Naturally, I didn't eavesdrop on their conversation."

Lipperstein again jotted down a note.

"It was Fell who discovered the body later?"

"Yes. He was with Mister Smith, one of our *Bishops*."

Lipperstein frowned. Featherstone explained:

"That's the nickname we give to those of our employees who are in charge of organizing tournaments."

"What can you tell me about this Fell?"

"Arthur Fell has been a member for several years." Featherstone paused for an instant. "I would say, at least seven or eight years. He's an excellent player, one of our best, in fact. He is a very calm and polite gentleman, always in a good humor. The poor man was quite shocked, and has been quite overwrought since. You may have seen him outside, at the entrance. He has been sitting on the steps since the macabre event, and has not budged since."

Lipperstein remembered seeing an old man whose gaze was lost in the distance when he arrived, and nodded.

"Very good. What else?"

Featherstone shrugged. "I'm afraid I can't be of much help for the rest. I had a cup of tea and returned to my office. I didn't leave it until I was informed of the discovery. Mister Smith might know more of what went on, I imagine."

"What do you mean, *you imagine?* Don't you have an idea about what your guests are doing?"

Featherstone sat up straight in his seat, on the defensive.

"Excuse me, Chief Inspector, but this is a place for relaxation. I don't see any reason that I should spy on those who come here. What's more," he continued, "between the guests and our *Bishops*, there might have been about fifty people here. I said, *I imagine,* because Mr. Smith was with Mr. Fell when they discovered the body. It occurred to me that he must have had a good reason to be there, that's all!"

Lipperstein was observing the publican, remaining impassive.

"Are you are suspecting me of being somehow involved in this horrible affair?" asked Featherstone.

"I have said no such thing," replied the Chief Inspector.

"Then, if you have finished with me, I would like to return to my other patrons, who are, for the most part, very distressed about all this."

Lipperstein made a courteous gesture.

"By all means, Mr. Featherstone. If I need you again, I will come and find you."

He stood up and held out his hand.

"Would you be kind enough to have Mr. Smith come in so that I can ask him some questions?"

The publican shook his his hand, nodded without saying a word, and left without closing the door. Lipperstein rose and went to stand in front of the window. His looked down toward the steps and saw the aforementioned Fell, still seated, his head between his hands. Around him, several men were trying to comfort him. The old man had poise, even in his distraught state. He sported a mop of beautiful grey hair, arranged with care, and wore a fashionable suit from Seville Row and beautiful leather shoes.

Lipperstein sighed; he understood the man's sorrow; he shared it. He had a lump in his stomach that wasn't going away. Who then would have wanted to kill Barry Barrison? He had turned that question over and over in his head, but no answer had come to him. In the almost ten years that he had been collaborating with the amateur sleuth, they had sent a great number of criminals to the gallows or put them behind bars together. The choice was, therefore, large.

Lipperstein was drawn from his thoughts by a discreet clearing of a throat. He turned around. A smallish man, in his thirties, stood near the table, stiff as a statue, his hands joined in front of him. He was dressed in the same livery as all of the *Bishops*: a dark uniform, white shirt and gloves. He had a juvenile face, brown hair and large, green, inquisitive eyes. Lipperstein went over to his chair and invited the young man to sit down across from him.

"Mister Smith, I suppose?" he asked, smiling.

The other man sat down, obviously ill at ease. "Yes, Chief Inspector," he replied in a not very confident voice. "Henry Smith."

"Relax, young man, I just need to go over a few details with you, just as you saw them, neither more, nor less."

"Yes, Sir, I understand. It's just that..."

"Yes?"

"I'm still in shock, you understand."

"Perfectly, young man. I can easily imagine how all this must be very upsetting. It is for me, too. But we don't have a choice, do we?"

Smith didn't reply. He twisted in his chair, ill at ease.

"Do you want a glass of water? A cup of tea?" asked Lipperstein.

"No, thank you, Sir. I prefer to do this as quickly as we can."

"All right. Then, I'm listening."

Lipperstein picked up his pen and waited.

"Where do you want me to start?"

"The beginning seems the most logical place, don't you think?"

Smith took a deep breath and relaxed a little.

"I arrived at seven-thirty, as I do every morning when I am working. At that early hour, there are very few people there. I drank a cup of tea with two colleagues and then we started setting up the grand salon. I consulted our agenda to see if any tournaments were planned for the day. There was only one of note for the afternoon. I believe that, given the circumstances, it will be cancelled."

Lipperstein interrupted him.

"You are telling me that *all* the games are planned in advance?"

"No, Sir," replied Smith. "Only those that count for the internal rankings at the club. The other games between the members aren't marked on the agenda. Several dozen of them take place every day. It would require a much bigger register to list them all."

Smith interrupted himself to ask, "May I be permitted to smoke, Sir?"

Lipperstein nodded. The *Bishop* took a pack of cigarettes out of his pocket and lit one. Then he continued:

"The first members began to arrive just after the opening, at eight. Sir Barry arrived at around eight-thirty, as he does every Sunday. First, he went to the bar to get a cup of tea, then and went to sit down at a little table near a window to read his paper. About an hour later, I saw that Mister Fell had joined him there. I don't know how long he'd been here. The two men were having a lively conversation. Mister Fell motioned to me and asked me to bring him a cup of tea; I hurried to comply."

"When you brought it to him, did you notice anything unusual?"

The *Bishop* blew out a puff of smoke and crushed the rest of his cigarette in an ashtray.

"No, Sir," he replied, after thinking for a moment. "Sir Barry and Mister Fell seemed to be cordial toward each other. These two had known each other for a long time, and they often engaged in heated exchanges on various subjects. I think they may have been discussing politics, but I'm not sure."

"All right," Lipperstein said impatiently. "What happened next?"

"Shortly thereafter, Sir Barry asked me if it would be possible to play a registered game in one of the rooms on the first floor, even thought it wasn't on the agenda."

"Was that a normal request?"

"Absolutely," acquiesced Smith. "This is one of our rules and everyone is asked to abide by it. In order for a game to be registered, of recorded, if you will, it's got to be listed on the agenda."

"Why?"

"Because in this case, it requires the presence of a third party to monitor and arbitrate the game, if necessary. So we must always have enough Bishops on stand-by to perform that task. I then went to ask for Mister Featherstone's authorization."

"Where was he?" interrupted Lipperstein.

"In his office. Sir Barry being one of our most well-known and oldest members, the request was granted at once. I was tasked with setting up the game. So I went up to the first floor to prepare H1."

"H1? What's that?"

"We have 32 rooms on the first floor. Each is named after a white square on the chessboard. H1 is the bottom square to the right."

Lipperstein sighed. "I see. What time was it then?"

"I would say, about ten o'clock, or not much later. After I was done, I went down to inform Sir Barry and

Mister Fell that the room was ready. The two men left the salon and I escorted them to the room."

"What did the preparation consist of?"

Smith shrugged. "Nothing too complicated or extraordinary. I placed a board on the table in front of the window, set up the pieces on it, and a clock next to it. I also put a log in the fireplace, in case those gentlemen wanted a fire. I brought in a pitcher of fresh water and two glasses, that I also placed on the table."

"Just water?"

"Yes. If one of the players want to order a drink, they have to order it from us, obviously. Otherwise, we provide only water." He paused again. "Speaking of which, I could use a glass myself, Sir. I have a dry throat."

"Of course. Go get one."

Smith got up, went across the long room to take a half-fill pitcher and two glasses out of a cupboard. He put on in front of the Chief Inspector and helped himself to some water. He continued after having drunk his glass.

"I stayed by the door, in case one of the two gentlemen needed anything. They sat down in the chairs in front of the fireplace and began to chat. Sir Barry asked me for some tea. I went down to the bar and returned with a pot and two cups. The two men were still talking. I poured the tea. Sir Barry then expressed the desire to be alone to concentrate on his opening moves before starting the game. I remember that Mister Fell teased him, telling him he was flattered that he considered him such a fearsome opponent. Mister Fell and I then left the room and returned downstairs."

"Did Sir Barry usually express the desire to be alone before a game?"

"Well, he sometimes did, as a matter of fact. He liked to be alone for a half hour to smoke and think."

Lipperstein jotted it down in his notebook.

"I then returned to my tasks while Mister Fell went to sit down again in the grand salon. I saw him take out a little notebook in which he started to write. After a while, he came to see me again, saying that he was concerned. He had returned to the first floor and had found the door of the room where they were supposed to play closed. After having called out to Sir Barry several times and not receiving any reply, he had come to ask for my help. We both went up. The door was, in fact, locked."

The Chief Inspector thought for a moment. "Continue, please."

"I tried several times to open it. I even hit it with my shoulder. Nothing worked. Mister Fell began to panic, calling out to Sir Barry, loudly and insistently. I then took it upon myself to break it down. It resisted my first attempt, although I heard the wood crack. I succeeded on my second attempt. Mister Fell rushed past me. I saw him turn pale when he reached the chair occupied by Sir Barry. He turned toward me and shouted for me to go get help."

Here, Smith stopped, his voice trembling.

"I found your man downstairs, who immediately took charge. I believe you know the rest, Chief Inspector."

Lipperstein stood up and put his hand on the young man's shoulder.

"Thank you, Mister Smith. I am finished with you for the moment. You are free to go."

The young *Bishop* stood up, bowed to Lipperstein, and left the room. The Chief Inspector looked at his watch. He slid his notebook back into his pocket and left the room. Eddings was waiting just outside.

"Do you want to see Mister Fell now?" he asked.

Lipperstein thought a moment.

"No, not yet. We are first both going to examine the room in detail, and you will tell me what you've found. Since Fell seems to be in a rather sorry state, I'll question him later. Send him home and tell him to rest."

Eddings nodded and added:

"Doctor Hilldale is waiting for you in the room. I'll go and tell Fell and be right back."

Lipperstein went down the corridor, ruminating his dark thoughts. The two policemen on guard had not budged. He saluted them briefly and entered the crime scene. The doctor was seated in front of the chessboard, mechanically playing with some of the pieces.

"You have examined the body, I suppose Doctor?" asked the Chief Inspector

The doctor rose, a sad smile on his lips. "Indeed I have, Chief Inspector. It was a sad duty."

"What did you find?"

The man stepped forward, limping, toward the armchair where Barry's body had been found.

"Not very much, I'm afraid. A single blow to the heart. Very little blood came out. Death was immediate."

"What about his position? How do you explain it? Why is he in such a restful position? Why did he not struggle?"

"I asked myself that question. Perhaps he was surprised while he was meditating? Or maybe the knife was thrown?"

Lipperstein approached the chair.

"Impossible, Doctor. Look: the chair is almost facing the fireplace. Only Barry's shoulder was facing the only window in the room. The murderer would have had to be a magician to succeed."

Eddings returned.

"Anything else, Doctor?" asked Lipperstein.

"Unfortunately, no. I would have loved to be able to tell you more."

"So be it then. If we need anything else from you, we will let you know. Leave your address with one of the officers below. Good day, Doctor."

The old Doctor, limping, picked up his briefcase and started toward the door, but stopped.

"Ah, yes, one more detail," he added, turning around. "The blow was very precise."

Lipperstein frowned. "What do you mean by *precise*?"

"Few people know exactly where the heart is located. All too often, they think it's too much to the left of the thoracic cage. Your murderer didn't."

He bowed to the two detectives and left the room. Lipperstein took out his notebook and put it on the chessboard.

"Your turn, Eddings," he began, without turning around, and scribbling a few notes quickly. "What did bother you?"

The young policeman scratched his head. "In the first place, the door, Guv," he answered.

Lipperstein turned around. "What about that door. It was stuck, wasn't it? That was the reason why Smith had to break it down."

"No, Guv. If Smith had to force it open, it was because if had been locked—from the inside. The key was on the little table next to Barrison."

Lipperstein went to the door. He leaned over and noticed that the lock was indeed engaged. He next looked at the floor. There was nothing there except for the pieces of wood that had scattered under the force of the *Bishop*'s blows. He straightened up.

"Why in God's name would Barry have locked himself in?"

"I don't know, Guv."

"There must be duplicates of that key?"

"No, Guv. I already asked. There are no duplicates or passkeys. Mister Featherstone want the members to be as much at ease as possible and not to be interrupted during their games."

"All right. What about the window? Did you find any traces that might indicate that someone got into the room that way?"

"Ah, that is odd too, Guv. You will notice that the window has not been forced. It was left open."

"Yes, and...?"

"I found no traces outside. The gutter is about three feet to the left. There's no evidence of it having been climbed."

Lipperstein went to the window, opened it wide and leaned out it to look outside. The garden spread out at his feet, superbly maintained. The gardeners were in the process of turning over the dirt in the large flower beds for new plantings. The lawn was very green. On his left he spotted the gutter in question.

"It wouldn't be easy to climb, but not altogether impossible for someone athletic enough."

"Except that..."

"What?"

"Look at the garden, Guv. Along the wall there is a pile of dirt. The gardeners are in the process of turning it over for the new plantings."

"Yes, I just saw that. It's a beautiful spot, and that garden is really well kept."

Eddings agreed. "The problem is that that pile of dirt is like ten feet wide and it was raked up not later than yesterday. You can still see the furrows formed by the rake."

Lipperstein frowned. "I see…"

The other man nodded. "Yes, Guv. There are no footprints in that dirt. He can't have come that way."

"Hmm. I suppose he couldn't have jumped over it and still reach the gutter, eh?"

"We have tried, Guv. It's impossible, unless you're a kangaroo. I also checked the access from the upper floors, and the roof. The window just above was closed from the inside. As for the roof, it's much too steep for anyone to try to climb down that way."

"But then, it means…" Lipperstein began.

Eddings looked at his boss straight in the eyes.

"Yes, Guv. It means that no one entered through the window, or the door. When Sir Barry was struck with that dagger, he was alone in a locked room."

4.

Lipperstein was back behind his desk. Since the Chief Inspector had returned to the Yard, he had had great difficulty concentrating. It had been a day charged with emotion. Barry Barrison's death had been difficult to accept, and even more so, given the circumstances. Usually, when a case was out of the ordinary,

Lipperstein called on the amateur sleuth to come to his help. Today, he couldn't.

It was the impossibility of the situation that kept him going. Even if he was at an impasse, he wasn't the type of man to get easily discouraged. If he had been promoted to Chief Inspector, it was because of his stubborn success in solving more cases than most at the Yard. But this time, without Barry's keen insights, he felt disarmed.

He knew he certainly could count on the help of Eddings and his team, but the amateur sleuth had had such a deductive mind that even the most tangled problems were like an open book to him.

Lipperstein was reminded of the many evenings they had spent at Tarford Manor before a fire trying solve a case together, him sitting in one of the two comfortable armchairs, listening to Barry, smoking his pipe, laying out his theories. The Chief Inspector was at first always skeptical, before being ultimately convinced by Barry's unstoppable logic. That was what characterized him: his extraordinary ability to notice the smallest detail, deemed insignificant by mere mortals, and to turn a seeming impossibility into an irrefutable proof of guilt.

Lipperstein got up, sighing, and went to stand in front of the window. That late afternoon, the view of the Thames was of no comfort to him. His heart was heavy. Someone knocked at the door.

"Come in," he answered.

Eddings appeared. The young detective remained on the threshold.

"Guv, I have told Mister Fell that you would call on him this evening to question him. He went home very depressed. Doctor Hilldale went to check on him and make sure he is all right. Will you want me to come?"

"What is the state of his health?"

"Stable, according to the Doctor."

"Well then, you should go home, Eddings Everything is all right. Be back tomorrow at eight. We'll have a briefing."

"All right. Good night, Guv!"

He closed the door, leaving Lipperstein lost in his thoughts. The Chief Inspector remained still for a moment; his eyes lost in the distance. His brain wandered from one thought to another. Nothing was normal in that affair. Not only was the victim unlikely, but there were so many inconsistent details that the whole case was a puzzle, the pieces of which could not be fitted together to make a coherent picture. The motive behind the crime simply escaped him. Not that Barry didn't have enemies—he did—but the circumstances which surrounded his murder were so strange that he didn't know where to begin.

Not even taking the trouble to close his office door, Lipperstein rushed out, got behind the wheel of his car and started driving. The London streets unfolded before his eyes one after the other. He drove like a robot, without thinking. It was fortunate that traffic was light, because otherwise he might have struck another vehicle, or a pedestrian.

The vehicle stopped in front of the gate of Tarford Manor. Lipperstein got out and looked at the always impressive dwelling. The Manor stood out silhouetted against the London skyline with the same elegance as its late resident. The Chief Inspector took a set of keys out of his pocket, then selected the right one. With a firm step, he went toward the entrance. It had been a long time since Alfred had opened the door for visitors. The old butler had been very affected by the death of Sir

Henry Tarford, his former employer. With him, he had lost the only family that he had known for years. However, Barry had succeeding in finding the right words to convince him to stay after he had leased the Manor. Relieved, Alfred had entered in the service of the amateur sleuth, being the only one, in his own eyes, capable of taking care of the ancestral dwelling. But the weight of the years, fatigue, and sickness, had finally taken their toll on the brave old servant and Alfred had passed away during the last winter.

After his death, Barry had refused to replace him. He had judged that only Alfred had been worthy of occupying that position. He had himself taken care of the Manor's upkeep, waiting for a proper Tarford heir to be located somewhere in America. His single-mindedness and attachment to the dwelling had been enough. The Manor, still resplendent, overshadowed all of the neighboring estates.

Lipperstein slipped the key into the keyhole and turned it. The door opened silently. The Chief Inspector remained undecided for a moment. Was this a good idea? His eyes looked into the entry hall. The sun had now set and there remained only a feeble twilight that was quickly disappearing over the horizon. The Manor was plunged into semi-obscurity. Silence reigned, weighing heavily on the Chief Inspector's soul.

After a last hesitation, Lipperstein went in and closed the door behind him. He felt a current of cold air and shivered. His eyes became accustomed to the obscurity. He took off his coat and hung it on the rack, as he did every time he came to visit. He was almost expecting to see Barry come out to greet him one of vigorous handshakes and to invite him to follow him into the large sitting-room.

Lipperstein shook his head to chase away those memories. He had come to try to find a clue that would allow him to know who might have murdered his friend. It was cold now—a real contrast with the mild weather that they had been experiencing for several days.

He cleared his throat, more to hear a reassuring sound than out of necessity. Tarford was in mourning. He had the feeling that the Manor understood what had happened at the Queen's Pawn, and that its occupant would no longer stroll about inside its walls. The Chief Inspector sighed; he had to pragmatic and not start imagining that the house had a soul and that it would react to Barry's passing...

He lit a candle and walked toward his late friend's office. If there was a place where he might find a clue, it was there. He turned into the corridor that led to the kitchen and reached for the doorknob of the door to Barry's office, which he opened with a single turn.

Despite the obscurity, the room was just as he remembered it, perfectly organized. The big mahogany desk was like a throne in the middle of the room. Behind it there was a brown leather armchair just waiting for someone to sit in it. A new wave of memories assailed him. Barrison usually sat there when he wrote, or walked up and down in front of the desk when he was telling him of his latest discoveries in an investigation.

Lipperstein stepped forward. The desk was in perfect order. The leather pad, the pen holder, the sheets of paper, everything was in its place. The Chief Inspector flipped through a pile of files sitting on the corner and rapidly read through the titles on the folders: *Experimental Graphology; Plants and Poisons—A Botanical Treatise of the Absurd; Common Madness: Labyrinth of Obscure Thoughts...* There were at least a dozen others, each dealing with a very particular subject. A sad smile floated on his lips. He recognized there the peculiar interests of the amateur sleuth. Several times, during their long conversations, Barry had tried to convince him of the necessity of reading this or that book.

To really understand a case, it's necessary to have the maximum number of facts at hand, whether you are a genius or not. Not being one myself, I try to be an assiduous reader and do my research, he liked to say.

Lipperstein let his eyes run over the bookshelves overflowing with books of every kind. Some of them were so old that they looked as if they were about to disintegrate. Others had bindings that were cracked in many places, indicative of frequent use.

Am I going to have to read all these books in order to understand what happened to you, Barry? Lipperstein wondered.

Lipperstein surprised himself by repeating that sentence aloud. There was a strange ambiance in the Manor, and hearing his own voice reassured him. He had less the impression of being alone.

"I am not like you, Barry," he continued aloud, walking up and down in front of the desk, his hands in his pockets. "I have neither the patience, nor the intelligence, to solve complex mysteries. You knew that well—I always need to have something tangible before my eyes in order to figure something out. That's the reason that our collaboration was..."

He interrupted himself, before continuing: "...so productive. Not that I am simple-minded—no—don't you misunderstand me. I learned a lot in your company. I think I'll be better able of grasping your methods in the future..."

He looked at the empty armchair.

"What should I do now? What would you do if you were here? I am sure you would already have pointed me in the right direction with one of your clever metaphors. That's what I need now..."

He sat in the empty chair and looked at the files.

"Who wanted to see you dead? And how did he do it? Did he scale that drainpipe without leaving any traces in the soil below? But how?"

He got up and began to pace.

"I have thought and thought about it, but I still don't see it. A circus artist—an acrobat, perhaps? But his task would still have remained incredibly difficult, with no room for error. Besides, you and I never arrested any acrobats before. Was it a gratuitous murder then? Or was it premeditated? Is there a rational explanation, or should I look at the supernatural?"

Lipperstein went to stand in front of the window. The moonlight was now bathing the Manor in a pale white light.

"Help me, Barry, please, " he finally said in a murmur.

"Then come and sit down, my friend, and let's talk."

The voice, hoarse and cavernous, came from behind him. Lipperstein made an about face. His jaw dropped and a shiver went down his spine. He tried to speak, but no sound came out of his mouth.

Seated comfortably in the leather armchair, a ghostly silhouette with hazy contours looked at the Chief Inspector with blue and piercing eyes.

Lipperstein immediately recognized the perfectly tailored suit and the haughty attitude. That ghostly form was none other than Barry Barrison.

Chief Inspector Harvey Lipperstein was not a coward. In a career of more than twenty years, he had encountered many strange situations, and had looked dispassionately at crime scenes that many people would have found abominable. But nothing had prepared him for the events of that fateful night. His mouth refused to close. His eyes remained fixed on the ghostly silhouette, seated and calm, which had been his friend.

Barry's ghost, meanwhile, stared at the Chief Inspector with his usual calm and questioning gaze as if he was expecting some kind of acknowledgement.

Slowly, Lipperstein stepped back, bumping against the window. He took out his service weapon and pointed it in the direction of the ghost. But the creature did not blink—or at least, it seemed so to him. Because of its absolute stillness, its contours undulated slightly like a piece of paper in a breeze wind.

Lipperstein forced himself to collect his senses, and to be calm. The very precepts that Barry had taught him during their years of collaboration now came back into his mind: *Don't rush to judgment, remain calm, breathe slowly, and examine the situation under every angle. Everything has an explanation, whatever it might be.* So he took a step forward, the barrel of his weapon still pointed in the direction of *that thing,* and said:

"What are you?"

"Don't be afraid."

Lipperstein had the impression that the words resounded throughout the Manor. They him in the stomach, squeezing his entrails in an icy grip. The voice was hoarse, glacial, and cavernous. A strange, unearthly odor escaped from the mouth of the ghost when it opened its mouth.

The Chief Inspector, more by pure defensive reflex than slow deliberation, fired twice. The shots went through the *thing* and hit the back of the armchair with a dull sound.

The ghost disappeared. Curls of what looked like smoke dispersed into the air, twisting on themselves for a few seconds—then, nothing.

Lipperstein gasped, then took another step forward, coming closer to the desk. The shots were indeed lodged in the back of the chair, at chest level. He looked all around, sweeping the room with his gaze and his gun. The unearthly odor had dissipated; the air was breathable again. He put down his gun on the desk and lowered his head. His heart became calmer. Obviously, he just had had a hallucination. Relieved, he closed his eyes a second. He thought he should leave the Manor. It had been a bad idea to come. He had thought that, by being here, he could soak up some of Barry's deductive powers, and solve the mystery of his friend's death. But the fatigue of the day and the sadness that he felt had betrayed him. He had a brief fit of nervous laughter.

Soak up his deductive powers? he thought. *Ha! It is rather his presence that almost soaked up my mind.*

He stood up straight and continued laughing without being able to stop. It was nervous anxiety. Finally, he managed to calm himself. His stomach was painful. And he was weeping. He felt the tears roll down his cheeks, but was unable to hold them back. He took another deep breath, put his weapon back in its holster, and looked sadly at the empty armchair in front of him.

"Good-bye, my friend," he said in a trembling voice. "May you rest in peace."

He would probably have to explain to his superiors why he had fired two shots into an empty chair, but that mattered little now. He had to leave. He stepped across the room and had his hand on the doorknob, when he heard:

"Stay. We need to talk."

Lipperstein became still again. Now, he recognized the voice and its intonation. There was no doubt. He turned around and again found himself facing the translucent silhouette of his late friend—except that this time, it was sharper and better defined. The face seemed more human and the eyes had pupils. The expression tried to be friendly, even if he perceived some infinite sadness and even a slight incomprehension in the vaporous eyes.

"Excuse me," the ghost said, *"but I must become used to my new condition."*

A smile formed itself on the ghostly face. Lipperstein swallowed.

"Barry? Is that you?"

The ghost replied in the affirmative.

"...Or more accurately," he added in a voice that was becoming more controlled and more natural, *"what I have become."*

The Chief Inspector took a step forward.

"By what devilish sorcery...?"

Barry shrugged.

"I don't know anything more about it than you do, even if I'm starting to have my idea about it."

Barry's ghost crossed his legs and took his pipe out of his pocket. He examined it carefully before putting it into his mouth.

"I wonder if..." he began.

He took a tobacco pouch from inside his jacket and placed it on the desk. He rummaged in another pocket, then in a third. Then a smile lit up his face. He pulled out a box of matches that he shook to check that it was not empty. Lipperstein heard the characteristic sound of the little pieces of wood hitting against each other. He shivered, not understanding much of what was happening.

"Are you going to stand there all night?" said Barry. *"We need to talk. So, take a seat and let's talk."*

The voice had now become almost human. The Chief Inspector then detected all the characteristics and intonations that Barry used, even that joking tone he liked to employ when he knew he was master of a situation. He rook a cautious step forward, looking for a chair.

"On your right, behind you," said the Ghost as he conscientiously filled his pipe.

Lipperstein automatically followed the directions. He no longer knew if he was dreaming or if he was awake. Should he flee, or sit down and talk with that ectoplasmic creature? Deep inside, he was sure he was at the point of tipping into madness. Suddenly, he gained a moment of clarity: he never thought he'd be so affected by Barry's death, and he definitely wanted to clear up the mystery, and see that his friend got justice. Perhaps this as the way to achieve it... He shrugged and sat down, facing the phantom, ready to make one last attempt at solving the puzzle before flipping to the other side of sanity.

He looked at his friend, who was in the process of lighting the bowl of his pipe. A thick cloud of white smoke floated briefly around the spectral face of the amateur sleuth before evaporating. Lipperstein sniffed; there was no smell of tobacco. He cleared his throat to give himself a confidence that he didn't feel.

"Barry? You must be aware that what you and I are experiencing right now cannot be real."

The ghost nodded. *"Well, this certainly seems beyond anything that you and I ever experienced. It is troubling."*

"Troubling?" replied Lipperstein, his voice rising. He moved about on his chair. "How witty! *Troubling!* Is that all you can find to say? I'm talking to a ghost, and all you have to say is, *it's troubling!*"

Barry frowned. In the same sepulchral voice, he replied, indignant, *"What would you say if you were in my place, Chief Inspector?"*

Under the force of his emotion, his face became deformed, appearing to flicker like a candle about to go out. Lipperstein remain glued to his chair, terrified. But the Ghost soon recovered and regained his human aspect.

"Please excuse me," he continued, as if nothing had happened, *"but I have not yet totally mastered my new condition. It seems that I must control my emotions or risk driving away my listeners."*

Lipperstein was short of breath. The transformation of Barry's face had frightened him. He thought he had seen evil, terror, fear, death and hatred materialize before him for a brief instant. His throat was dry. He wanted to answer, but no word came out of his mouth.

"Are you all right?" asked Barry.

Lipperstein shook his head. He finally replied in a hesitating voice:

"Not really, but do get a hold on of yourself, Barry! I'm not certain that I can endure a second time what I just saw."

Barry moved about on his chair. *"Yes, I understand. I shall learn to control this..."*

101

"Good! Now tell me how..." Lipperstein began.

"*How did I end up like this? I don't know, not really.*"

"But you do know what happened to you?"

"*Yes. I am dead, I'm a ghost, that's obvious,*" Barry answered, exhaling a new cloud of odorless smoke. "*But for the rest, I'm counting on you.*"

"So you *are* a ghost... By Jove! Otherwise, yes, I can confirm that you died this morning."

"*Where did that happen?*"

"At the *Queen's Pawn*."

"*In which room?*"

"How do you know that you died in a room?"

"*Because it couldn't have happened in any other way. I imagine that I didn't die of natural death. I am— or should I say, I was—in perfect health. So I must have been murdered. A quiet place is to commit a successful murder. The grand salon is too exposed, always full of people. The second floor? No tournaments are planned for the next month or so. So I deduct that my body...*" Here, he stopped for a moment, realizing the strangeness of his words. "*...My body must have been found in one of the private rooms of the first floor.*"

He remained pensive for a moment, then continued:

"*I don't remember anything beyond leaving the Manor to go to the* Queen's Pawn. *It's strange, especially for me, because I never forget the smallest detail, no matter how insignificant.*"

That time, Lipperstein had no doubt. As unbelievable as that might be, it really was Barry Barrison who sat in front of him. That made him feel calmer, even though he would have been hard pressed to explain why in a rational manner.

"You always had a very sharp mind," he said.

"*Thank you, but I don't know if that should reassure me or frighten me.*"

Lipperstein suddenly burst out laughing. "Jesus! Look at me! What's happened to me! I am discussing a murder with a ghost! How is that even possible?"

"*You called me.*"

Taken aback, Lipperstein replied, "Called? You mean, like I conjured you up? Is that what you're saying?"

Barrison smiled. "'*Help me, Barry, please,*'" he repeated in a voice perfectly mimicking that of Lipperstein. "*Those were your words, weren't they?*"

The Chief Inspector hesitated, troubled once more by the changes in the Ghost's voice.

"Maybe," he answered, scratching his head. "I'm no longer sure."

"*Well, I answered that call, whether it was deliberate or not.*"

Lipperstein remained incredulous. "So I invoked you?"

"*In some way, yes.*"

"But how is that possible?"

"*I don't know. I admit that is beyond my current understanding, too. It is only a hypothesis, mind you.*"

Lipperstein shrugged. He smiled at his friend. "Well, nothing more can surprise me now."

Barry smiled back. "*I was invited to a séance once, in this very Manor, in fact. You were, too. If you remember, it was a pretext for murder, but afterward, I confided in you that, despite my disbelief, I had been troubled by what I had felt. Perhaps I was touched by the supernatural without being aware of it?*"

"But why? For what reason?"

Barry shrugged. *"How would I know? That is only another hypothesis."*

Lipperstein looked at the Ghost of his friend up and down. He rubbed his eyes, but the ectoplasmic creature did not disappear.

"I'm going to dismiss the notion I have stumbled into madness and accept that you are in some fashion real, even if you're a ghost. For the moment, what you are, or why, is not important. Do you think you can help me solve..." He paused. "...Your own murder?"

For the first time, a veil of doubt obscured Barry's ghostly eyes, and Lipperstein read a doubt there.

"Yes, of course. Perhaps that is why I am here."

The Chief Inspector swept away the matter with a wave of his hand. "Good. Where shall we begin then?"

Barry thought for a moment, then replied:

"Let's start at the beginning. Tell me about your day."

Lipperstein settled comfortably into his seat. As strange as that may have seemed a few minutes ago, he now felt himself truly at ease for the first time that day. He began his recitation of facts, forcing himself to be as precise as possible. He related every detail, every word as faithfully as he could remember them. Barry had put his pipe down on the desk, joined his hands under his chin, closed his eyes, and listened to his story with great attention. When the Chief Inspector was finished, the sleuth looked him straight in the eye.

"I see that, despite your emotional involvement, you still managed your investigation with the same minute attention to details."

The other man smiled. "I will take that as a compliment, Barry."

"You should. What do you intend to do next?"

"Tomorrow, I intend to question Arthur Fell at the Yard. He's the only one left I haven't questioned yet."

"*Good. What about the room? Do you intend to examine it again?*"

Lipperstein moved about on his seat. "Why? Do you think I might have missed something?"

"*Not you. Based on what you have told me, you haven't examined the room at all.*"

"True. It's Eddings who took care of that, but I have complete confidence in him."

"*I'm not sure I do. According to your story, I died alone, stabbed precisely in the heart. The door was locked—by me! The window, however, was open. My position in relation to it made any shot from the outside impossible. Further, your own examination shows that, unless it was performed by an acrobat endowed with supernatural powers, it would have been impossible for someone to have come in that way by way of the drainpipe without leaving any trace.*"

Barrison paused.

"*Under these conditions, my Cartesian mind tells me that you need to re-examine every aspect of the situation. You missed something. There are no such things an impossible murder.*"

Lipperstein looked at the Ghost. He was right. And that was undoubtedly what had been bothering him all day.

6.

Lipperstein opened his eyes, taking in a big gulp of air. He was sitting at his desk in his office at the Yard. He felt tired and stiff. He straightened and stood up, cracking his joints. \He looked at the clock on the wall.

It was 6:47 a.m. Had he dreamed the events of the night before? He walked around his desk and went to stand in front of the window. His glance went over Waterloo Bridge. The morning fog enveloped the majestic monument in a cocoon-like cloak.

Lipperstein was certain that he hadn't dreamed up anything. The last time he had looked at the bridge, the sun was still shining. It had been late Sunday afternoon. Now, it was Monday morning. What had happened the day before slowly unfurled in his head, right up to his visit to Tarford Manor, and his encounter with Barry's Ghost the night before. He was sure it had not been a dream.

He passed a hand over his face; he was not shaved. So he had not gone home. A look at his clothes confirmed it. He was wearing the same suit as the day before, and the same shirt. It was only his tie that he was not wearing—but he had no recollection of what he had done with it.

Trembling, he turned toward the little table that held the tea kettle. He poured himself a large cup and drank rapidly from it. The tea was cold.

He asked himself, how long he had been in the office before he woke up? What had he done after his conversation with the Ghost? Why did he no longer remember the end of that terrifying day?

Motivated by a sense of urgency, he searched the pockets of his suit to check that he had all his personal effects. Nothing was missing. He went over to his desk and opened the first drawer. His service weapon was there. He picked it up and checked the cylinder. Two empty cartridges. The two shots he had fired resounded in his head. He remembered seeing the ectoplasmic figure evaporate under the impact of the bullets.

He put the gun back in the drawer and glanced over his desk. Everything was not in a tidy pile—that was not like him. The Chief Inspector loved order and clarity. His workspace was usually as clean and well organized as his ideas. But this morning, he had to admit he was no longer sure about anything. Several of his most intimate convictions about Life and Death had been shaken the night before.

Lipperstein returned to his seat to try to organize his thoughts. He remained still, his face in his hands, turning and poring over his recollections in his cloudy mind. He grew concerned. Since his sudden awakening, he experienced a sense of powerlessness such as he had never known before. Nothing in this case was natural. The circumstances of Barry's death were strange. And what to think about his ghost?

The Chief Inspector tried to remember what the Ghost had said on that subject. He had mentioned a previous séance which he had attended, or almost attended? He remembered the case now—the attempted murder of Sir Henry Tarford, and that odd Austrian Countess, Brunhild von Wachter, which wasn't even really Austrian... And even if that was somehow pertinent, what relationship did it have with the Ghost now haunting Tarford Manor?

He didn't know, and he detested that feeling: *Ignorance is the attribute of the weak,* he had learned during his years at the Yard, and Lipperstein didn't consider himself weak. He had suffered too much during his youth before joining the force.

He stood up and left his office. Given the early hour, he was alone. He decided to go home, change and freshen up. With a determined step, he went down the stairs four at a time, climbed into his car and drove off.

It was just before 10 a.m. when Eddings knocked at his superior's door.

"Come in," responded the firm voice of Lipperstein.

The young detective opened the door and went into the office. The Chief Inspector was seated behind his desk, busy filing a stack of notes scratched on the pages of his notebook. He addressed his subordinate without even taking the time to look up.

"Is Fell here?"

"Yes, Guv," answered Eddings, without saying good morning.

Eddings was used to Lipperstein's changing moods, even if he had not worked under him for long. He understood how the mind of his superior worked, even if he'd been a little surprised at first.

"Would you like me to bring him in?"

Lipperstein nodded. Eddings left, to return a few minutes later accompanied by an older man with an imposing presence, who moved slowly.

The Chief Inspector stood up and came to meet the visitor. He had changed, shaved closely, and wore a new tie.

"Mister Fell, I presume?"

"Professor Arthur Fell, to be precise," the man completed in a serious and warm voice, with a pronounced guttural accent. "And" he added, with a smile, "a professor who has stopped teaching due to his age."

The two men exchanged a warm handshake and Lipperstein invited the professor to sit down in the chair he had placed in front of the desk. Then he motioned to Eddings, who left the room, closing the door behind him. The Chief Inspector took his place again behind his desk. He examined the old professor. From all evidence, the man was impressive. He wore long salt and pepper hair arranged with care. It was coiffed in a complicated style, mingling madness and genius. Little, round glasses did nothing to hide a steely gray gaze surmounted by brushy eyebrows. The thin, wrinkled face showed profound intelligence. As for his dress, it was perfect: a gray suit white shirt, and patent leather shoes.

"Professor Fell, I am sorry to have had to ask you to come here under such sad circumstances," Lipperstein began.

"Call me Arthur, please," said Fell, motioning with his hand, and sitting down.

Lipperstein smiled. "I prefer to stick to protocol, if you don't mind."

Fell nodded.

"Could you tell me your version of what happened yesterday, Professor?" continued the Chief Inspector

Fell steepled his fingers and frowned.

"Where do I begin?... It is very complicated. I thought all night about what happened, and I doubt that this is your first interview. I arrived at the *Pawn* at about eight thirty, or a little thereafter; I don't remember exactly."

"Do you usually arrive so early?"

"Yes. I have been a widower for almost twenty years. I have neither a family nor a child. My only occupation and my single passion since I retired from teaching is chess. I therefore go to the club as often as possible. During the week-ends, the doors open a little earlier than during the week. That's a godsend for an old man like me," he concluded, his eyes shining.

Lipperstein raised an eyebrow.

"You said you used to be a teacher, correct? I can picture you in a white coat with test tubes, everyone more dangerous than the other, trying to concoct I don't know what miracle formula..."

Fell had a short laugh.

"That wasn't me at all! I admit—with some embarrassment—that I was always rather bad in science at university. No, it is the human brain that has always fascinated me."

"You were a surgeon?"

Fell burst out laughing.

"Absolutely not! Pardon me for laughing; I don't mean any disrespect to you, Chief Inspector. I was rather imprecise with my words. When I spoke of the human brain, I meant its connections, what allows us to think, to reflect, to analyze, also to deceive ourselves, sometimes... My specialty is psychiatry. I have studied and taught the masters: Joseph Breuer, Wilhelm Fliess, and Sigmund Freud. Perhaps some of these names are familiar to you already?"

Lipperstein shook his head negatively.

"You said you had retired from teaching?"

"Yes, some years ago, already, but I continue to read and stay abreast of progress. It's a fascinating field, you know."

"I believe you, Professor, but I suppose that's not our concern right now. Let's return to the matter at hand, please."

"So, when I arrived, I went to the grand salon to get a cup of tea. I saw that Barry was already there, so I invited myself to his table."

"How long had you known Sir Barry?"

Fell thought for a moment and adjusted his glasses.

"I can't say precisely. Ten years, at least, perhaps more."

Lipperstein took some notes in his notebook.

"How did you make his acquaintance?"

"At a charity tournament organized by the club. We chatted afterward. I greatly admired his knowledge of the game. He was truly a remarkable man. After that, we played regularly together. Barry was an extraordinary player, with much knowledge of the noble game."

Fell relaxed a little and crossed his legs.

"I was lucky to be invited for dinner a few times at Tarford Manor, and we often talked until the early hours of the morning."

"What did you talk about that morning after you sat at his table?"

"Everything and nothing. That was what was fascinating about Barry. The most trivial subjects could turn into a passionate conversation!"

Lipperstein was becoming impatient. He put down his pencil and looked the professor straight in the eyes.

"What led you to that fatal game?"

Arthur Fell lost his haughty attitude. He shrunk down a little in his chair.

"A stupid war of ego between two bored men, I confess. We were discussing various theories about openings and we were having a disagreement about a certain opening. Our discussion got more heated—while remaining courteous—and so, we decided to test our respective opinions by playing a series of games." Fell sighed sadly. "It was as simple as that," he concluded.

Lipperstein continued to write frenetically in his notebook.

"Mister Smith then set up the private room according to your instructions, is that right?"

"Yes, room H1, to be precise."

"Did you notice anything unusual there?"

"No, nothing at all. We stayed below to finish our drink during the time it took for the *Bishop* to do the set up. We didn't get up to the first floor until the room was ready."

"I meant, in the room, itself—nothing there seemed unusual to you?"

Fell thought for a moment.

"Not that I recall. The room was set up like all the others: the chessboard, the two armchairs, the fireplace with a log inside, the pitcher of water... I've thought about it thoroughly and I can't remember anything out of the ordinary." He paused. "Unless... Even so, there was one detail, negligible perhaps..."

Lipperstein sat up straight in his chair.

"It was quite cold in the room. I remember that I shivered when we entered."

Lipperstein jotted down a note.

"Did you notice whether the window was open or closed?"

"I admit that, at the time, I didn't pay much attention to the window, but thinking about it, I think that it was open."

"Was that unusual?'

"It all depends on the season, really. Still, even if we had a lot of sun yesterday, the temperature outside was rather cool."

"All right, what happened then?"

"Mister Featherstone came in to ask us if everything was all right."

"At what time was that?"

"I didn't look at my watch. Nine o'clock? Nine thirty perhaps? I can't say exactly."

"All right. Please, continue."

"We sat down, Barry and I, in front of the fireplace and drank another cup of tea that Smith had brought us. Then Barry asked to be alone a moment to reflect. I admit that I teased him a little then, to shake his concentration."

"Was that usual?"

"Rather. Geniuses can be odd, you know, and Barry was definitely a genius. So I left him alone in the room and went down to the grand salon to wait." Fell paused. "What followed, you already know," he concluded.

"But I'd like to hear it from your point of view, Professor."

"All right. Some time passed. Not seeing Barry return downstairs to tell me he was ready, I began to wonder what he was doing. So I went back upstairs and knocked at the door. I didn't get an answer. I knocked again. I called out. Nothing. Even if Barry could behave oddly on occasion, that was very unusual—even for him. So I returned downstairs and asked Smith to come up, sharing my concerns. We both stopped in front of the door. He knocked. Still no I convinced him to break the door down. That wasn't easy and it took him several attempts to do it..."

Here, Fell stopped again. His hands were trembling. His eyes were shining. He passed his tongue over his lips several times.

"When the door finally broke, I rushed into the room," he continued. "I felt very cold. I went quickly to the armchair where Barry was sitting. What I saw there left me momentarily speechless, bit I quickly got control of myself. I shouted to Smith, who had remained on the threshold, to go and fetch a doctor, bit in truth, I knew it was already too late."

Fell's eyes were now filled with barely contained emotion.

"I had seen the blade of a dagger, plunged up to the guard, sticking out of my friend's chest!" he concluded.

7.

Lipperstein was pacing in his office. The conversation that he just had had with Fell supported the suggestion that Barry's Ghost had made to him the night before. He had to return to the *Queen's Pawn* and go through that little room with a fine-tooth comb. The answer was there, but to find it, he needed to have a clear mind.

He left his office and hailed his subordinate.

"Eddings! Come with me to the *Pawn*. I want to take another look at the crime scene!"

The young man raised his head, puzzled.

"Why? Did I miss anything?"

"I don't know yet. I'd like to form my own opinion. Is that room still locked?"

"Yes. It will remain so until you order it otherwise. No one has been in there."

"Excellent! Let's go."

Without waiting, Lipperstein was already heading down the stairs.

The two detectives arrived at their destination a half-hour later. The dullness of that sinister day only added to that heavy and sad atmosphere that surrounded the club. The two men entered. The death of one of their own—and not the least of them—still weighed heavily on all the members present.

They were greeted by one of the *Bishops,* who took their coats, still damp from the fog. Without hesitation, Lipperstein went into a hallway to his left and stopped in front of a door with a metallic plaque on which was inscribed in gold letters: *William Featherstone, Mgr.* He knocked and entered without waiting for a response.

Behind his desk, Featherstone, surprised, closed a thick book with a leather cover.

"Chief Inspector?" he inquired.

He opened one of the desk drawers to his right and slid the thick volume into it.

"I would like to see the salon where Sir Barry's body was found," said Lipperstein.

"Surely you don't need my authorization for that?"

The manager straightened up; Lipperstein sensed some defiance in the tone of his answer.

"Correct," he said, smiling, "but I was hoping for your presence at my side."

"Whatever for, if I may ask?"

Featherstone stood up and readjusted the vest of his dark suit.

"Perhaps a detail will come back to you, something that may have seemed insignificant at the time, but may have acquired a particular importance since."

The manager walked around his desk and came to stand in front of the Chief Inspector. He smiled back.

"Very well! I'll be happy to do it, of course, but if you don't mind my saying so, your request seems as little morbid to me."

The Chief Inspector stepped aside to allow him to go out first.

"Yes, you may well be right, but everything about this business seems morbid to me."

The two men caught up with Eddings, who had been waiting at the foot of the stairway leading to the first floor. The young policeman was in the company of Smith and Sir Geoffrey Hilldale, the doctor who had examined Barry's body, and whose presence Lipperstein had requested.

The group climbed the stairs, Eddings leading the way.

Once they reached the door of the private room where the amateur sleuth had been murdered, Eddings stepped aside. Lipperstein stopped on the threshold. He looked at the crime scene, caressing his mustache. Then he turned around and addressed the others.

"Gentlemen, I'm going to ask you to remain here while I examine the room in detail."

He stepped inside the room, pushing the broken door open.

"I hope that this isn't going to take too long," said Featherstone to Eddings. "I have a number of things to do."

"Don't worry, Sir. The Chief Inspector just needs a few minutes alone in there. It's in those moments, you see, that he is the most effective."

"Really? Well, I hope that will prove true today."

"Do you have an idea of what he is looking for?" asked Doctor Hilldale.

The older man seemed tired. His face was drawn, as if he had not slept the night before. Eddings didn't know how well Barry Barrison and Hilldale knew each other, but the doctor seemed quite affected by the sleuth's death.

"Some kind of detail that is out of the ordinary, I suppose. I myself examined the room yesterday, but I don't have his experienced eye."

The doctor nodded. Eddings glanced at Smith. The young *Bishop* remained silent, his hands crossed in front of him. He seemed nervous. His face had become slightly flushed when Lipperstein had announced that he wanted to go into the room alone. His fingers were pale at the joints from his twisting them frenetically.

Inside, Lipperstein had an inspiration. He emptied his mind of every idle thought and distraction, and concentrated just on the room. He kneeled down and examining the hinges of the door. The wood had broken under Smith's blows. There were still some broken pieces on the floor, lying about in a large perimeter. The impact had to have been violent. He then approached the lock and examined it. Although not an expert, he didn't spot any suspicious scratches, other than those caused by normal use, but it didn't rule out the notion that the lock may have been picked from the outside. He heard Eddings' voice coming from the outside, but blocked it out.

He stood up and walked toward the fireplace. The chessboard with its thirty-two pieces was still in place, on a separate table. The pieces were positioned in a symmetrical manner on each side. Lipperstein picked the two black horsemen, looked at them, then put them back on their original squares, facing their adversaries. The clock next to the board had both hands pointing to twelve—nothing irregular.

The Chief Inspector went to the open window, and for the first time, he felt the cold and humidity that had seeped into the room. Stooping down, he noticed some thin brown scratches on the floor. He took out his notebook and jotted down a few notes. He then got down on his hands and knees and placed his cheek against on the floor, remaining still for several seconds. If it hadn't been for the gravity of the situation, it would almost have been comical. He finally stood up, wincing, cursing his aching joints.

Finally, he turned toward the two comfortable armchairs placed in front of the fireplace. He couldn't hold back a shiver—which had nothing to do with the cold—remembering the sight of his dead friend, still very clear in his mind. On the little table were the two cups of tea, two glasses, the jug of water, and the key that opened the room.

Lipperstein picked it up and returned to the door. He put the key in the lock and turned it. The lock turned into the open position without any sound. He took out the key and examined it closely, going to the window to take advantage of the light. He didn't notice anything unusual about it. The metal was cold to the touch. He blew on it: small fragments of dust came loose from the base of the key. Nothing else.

He went back to the two armchairs and examined the one in which Barry had been sitting. With a gesture he had so often repeated during his career, he plunged his hand into the space created by the two cushions that covered the chair. His fingers felt nothing but the supporting wood of the back. He straightened up again, puzzled. His glance went then to the small table. The cups still bore faint traces of the tea. He picked up one of the two glasses, smelled it, then put it back.

In the hearth, he noticed a log that had not had time to burn up. There were no ashes, no cinders. Everything was spotless clean. Too clean, perhaps? The Chief Inspector frowned. He picked up his notebook, that he had left by the chessboard, then stopped, became still, his eyes staring into the distance. He added some words inside before putting it back into his pocket. He then started toward the door, that he opened slowly.

"Come in, Gentlemen. My apologies for having kept you waiting for so long."

One after the other, the three men stepped into the room. Eddings remained on the threshold, his arms crossed, leaning on the doorframe.

"What do you want from us, Chief Inspector?" asked Featherstone in an irritated voice. "You're the detective, not us."

Without taking the trouble to answer, Lipperstein went toward Eddings, whom he took into the corridor. He whispered few words into his ear, and the young man disappeared.

Smith had preferred to stay to one side, near the door. Doctor Hilldale had gone to the armchairs, taking care to avoid the one where Barry had lain and sitting in the other, breathing heavily.

"I don't know, Mister Featherstone," answered the Chief Inspector laconically. "Perhaps examining the room anew will bring about some kind of recollection?"

"I doubt it," answered the manager, quickly.

"How can you be so sure? You have only come in—unless you were here before?"

Featherstone became still.

"No, absolutely not," he defended himself, "but I know these rooms by heart. I'm the one who bought the furnishings. They're all the same. This one is no different from the others!"

"In no way at all?"

Featherstone finally seemed to look at what he saw around him. He scrutinized the room with a circular motion. He paused for a moment when his eyes reached the chair where Barry had sat. Then he shook his head.

"No, I'm sorry, I really don't see anything different."

"What about you, young man?"

The question was addressed to Smith, who had lowered his eyes and was looking at his feet, trying hard to be ignored.

"I agree with Mister Featherstone, Sir."

"It was you who set up the game, right?"

"Yes, Sir. Sir Barry sat with his side to the fireplace, and Mister Fell was facing him near the window, as per our tradition."

"Tradition? What tradition?"

"It's more a custom than a tradition," interrupted Featherstone, who was becoming impatient. "White always sits with his side to the fireplace. It's a custom—a whim of our members. What the Devil! Why does it matter? You should be busy finding Sir Barry's murderer instead of asking silly questions to my staff."

"But that is precisely what I am doing, Sir, I assure you," answered Lipperstein.

The peremptory tone used by the Chief Inspector created an uncomfortable silence in the room. Featherstone went to lean against the mantel of the fireplace, in a pose that made him seem important.

"What about you, Doctor?" continued Lipperstein, in a level voice. "Has anything occurred to you?"

The older man shook his head. Since he had sat down in the armchair, his gaze had become fixed, almost unwillingly, on the other armchair in front of him. He remained silent, as if lost in his thoughts, as if he were reliving a scene that had traumatized him. The Chief Inspector reluctantly sat down across from him and put his hand on his knee.

"Doctor Hilldale?" he asked.

The old man finally seemed to come out of his wide-awake nightmare.

"Excuse me," he said in a strained voice, clearing his throat. "No, I don't see anything unusual. As a frequent player, I know these rooms like the back of my hand, as does our host," he continued, with a gesture in the direction of Featherstone. "And I freely admit that I see nothing out of the ordinary here. I am very sorry not to be more helpful to you—or our late friend."

"*A fortiori*—and excuse me for stirring painful memories—nothing seemed abnormal to you when you examined Sir Barry?" asked Lipperstein, forcing himself to be calm.

"It was, I think, the least complicated post-mortem that I ever had to perform in my entire career. God preserve me from having to do another one!" His voice had recovered its strength. "Why was Barry's posture so relaxed? Why had so little blood escaped from the wound? Why was there a total absence of struggle? Everything seemed so *strange*..."Here, he paused. "But in the end, there is nothing that medicine can't explain," he concluded, with a strangled voice.

Lipperstein addressed the three men.

"Gentlemen, thank you for your assistance. I am finished with you for the moment. If I have more questions, Mister Eddings will contact you."

He went to the door and made a courteous parting gesture. Smith went out first, his head still lowered. Featherstone followed, stiff as a post. The old doctor got up from the armchair as well as he could, and left last, limping. He placed his hand on Lipperstein's arm and said:

"Please find who did it."

And he left.

Left alone, Lipperstein looked one last time at the room.

"I promise you that, Doctor," he said aloud, "but to do that, I must have another discussion with my new friend, the ghost…"

He closed the door and went down the stairs with a firm step.

8.

The next day, Chief Inspector Lipperstein went to Deception Alley, a grungy little street located in one of the most destitute quarters of London. He was accompanied by Eddings and a dozen of his men.

The Chief Inspector had assembled his team earlier, informing them of the imminent arrest of Barry Barrison's murderer. After that short briefing, two police cars headed in the direction of Bloomsbury, accompanied, to Eddings' great surprise, by an ambulance from St Mary Bethlehem Hospital, a.k.a, Bedlam, the notorious psychiatric hospital. Lipperstein had remained silent on the subject when Eddings had questioned him, assuring his subordinate that the presence of qualified medical personnel would be indispensable for what would ensue.

When the three vehicles arrived at the little street, Lipperstein told his team to surround one of the buildings, No. 18B, to avoid any flight through one of the back windows. As for Eddings, he was assigned to watch the street in order to stop any neighbors who would eventually want to approach too closely.

Lipperstein advanced toward the door, accompanied by three policemen and two orderlies. Eddings saw the door open, and the little group rushed through the opening. Cries and shouts soon were heard from the modest dwelling; then there was calm.

A few minutes later, Lipperstein came out, followed by the policemen. As for the orderlies, they were hauling an individual strapped in a strait jacket who was gesticulating and shouting in a high voice. Eddings let escape an astonished swear word when he recognized the prisoner. He let the little group pass and approached his superior officer.

"Are you certain that he is the one, Guv?"

Lipperstein looked at him gravely. "I no longer have any doubt, Eddings."

Faced with the questioning look of his subordinate, Lipperstein continued:

"Let's return to the Yard and I'll explain everything to you."

The two men got back in the police car and were driven back to their office. Lipperstein closed his eyes, relieved. His thoughts turned back to the previous night as he remembered the conversation that he had had with Barry's ghost...

After leaving the *Pawn,* Lipperstein had first returned to his office to pick up some notes and various documents. He had let Eddings know that he would not be back that evening, but made it clear that he counted on each of them to come in early the next morning, and that the day would be very busy.

He had then taken a cab, not wanting an official car to be seen parked near a bar, and had gone to sit at a table in a quiet pub located just behind Tarford Manor. Not knowing his ectoplasmic friend's schedule, he had decided to wait until nightfall while sipping a pint. He would take advantage of this time to put his notes in order.

Around ten-thirty, he lifted his head from his notebook, now full of pages of scribbled notes. He paid for his drinks and left. The night was cool and clear. A little breeze carried in its wake some litter strewn along the sidewalk. Once in front of the Manor, Lipperstein looked to his right and left; he was alone in the street. Even if he knew he could explain his presence here, being a Scotland Yard detective, he preferred that his entrance go unnoticed. He did not want to be interrupted in the middle of his conversation by a bobby summoned by a zealous neighbor.

Lipperstein unlocked the door and pushed it. He entered the vestibule and shut the door behind him. He was struck by the change in temperature: it was cold inside. In spite of feeling some doubt, he went straight straight to the office. His eyes, now accustomed to the dim light, enabled him to walk without stumbling. He hesitated a little before pushing the door open. He wasn't certain of what he had experienced the night before. Perhaps he had fantasized his encounter with the Ghost? Finally, he put his hand on the doorknob and entered

On the other side of the desk, he saw a silver-white cloud. He stood where he was, transfixed by the sight, not daring to move, content to wait. As if the entity had noticed his presence, the spirals of smoke began to move in a complicated skein. The empty spaces disappeared, one after the other, and the cloud began to change form, as if shaped by some invisible hands. When the transformation was complete, the now identifiable silhouette of Barry Barrison, seated in his armchair, his legs crossed, appeared. His face was calm, almost relaxed, and broke apart with a smile.

"*Happy to see you again, my friend,*" the Ghost began, with a voice that sounded firmer than the night before. "*Sit down! If you have returned, it's because you have some new information to share with me.*"

Lipperstein finally stepped forward and put his pile of documents on the desk. He held out his hand to Barry, then, realizing the futility of the gesture, sat down.

"*Ah, yes, I'm sorry that we shall no longer be able to exchange cordial handshakes,*" said the sleuth in an almost light tone. "*You and I are going to have to learn new habits, but we will discuss it later. There are more urgent things to be taken care of...*"

He moved forward on his seat and placed his ghostly hands on the desk as he usually did.

"*So? Have you reexamined the room as I suggested?*"

"I have, this morning, in the company of Inspector Eddings, Mister Featherstone, young Mister Smith and Doctor Hilldale."

"*Excellent. I'm listening.*"

Barry sat back, crossed his hands under his chin, and closed his eyes. Lipperstein then recounted in detail his recent visit to the *Pawn*. The Ghost remained silent for while after the Chief Inspector had finished his report. Lipperstein moved about on his chair.

"Does any of this mean anything to you, Barry? I confess I'm just as much in the dark as I was before."

Barry opened his eyes.

"*Do you have a copy of the pages of that big leather book?*" he asked.

Lipperstein looked through the files and placed them in front of his friend.

"Here they are. I admit I found Featherstone's behavior rather queer. I surprised him in his office removing a dozen pages from that book. I tortured my mind to try to understand what they could be about, until I had an idea. That must be a membership log, where all the personal information about those who belong to the club is kept. Later, I discreetly asked Eddings to go and take a look at it, and to, er, borrow the pages concerning the protagonists of this affair, and replace them with blank sheets of paper so the switch wouldn't be noticed right away. I read them when we returned to the Yard, but I confess that I didn't find very much of interest in there. Smith owes some gambling debts, Hilldale is getting a little forgetful, and Fell has a chronic bronchitis that requires medication at regular intervals. Obviously, Featherstone is a busybody who likes to know everything about everyone."

He placed the pages in front of Barrison.

"There is an amusing detail. I learned that you were a dedicated philatelist."

Barry smiled slightly.

"Not really, no. I find stamp collecting too basic and simplistic a pastime. Normally, I like to keep things in my life private. But I suspected—and you just proved it—that Featherstone kept records about all of the club members, so I made sure he had something harmless to write about me."

Lipperstein smiled. There was again proof of his friend's ingenuity and mental acuity!

Barry pored over the pages. Not being able to touch them, he asked Lipperstein to turn them as he read. He stopped on one record that he reread several times. He finally stood up and began to pace behind the desk in silence. Lipperstein knew that it was his friend's way to review and analyze the information in his head. What bothered him was that he could no longer hear the sound of the amateur sleuth's footsteps! That was both logical and yet disturbing.

Long minutes went by. Lipperstein, hypnotized, followed his friend with his eyes. Barry finally stopped and turned toward the Chief Inspector. He had come to a conclusion.

"*How was the soil at the bottom of the window?*" he asked

"Well, it was damp and of the same consistency as that found in the rest of the garden."

"*Was it compact?*"

"No, it was made up of fine particles. Why?"

"*Then it would have stuck to the bottom of any shoe. And if it had, you would have found traces of it inside.*"

"I suppose so."

"*The whole thing was meant to lead you astray, and make you believe that my murderer had entered the room by way of the window.*"

"I did, in fact, believe that." Lipperstein paused, perplexed. "Since the door was locked from the inside, the murderer had to enter through the window, didn't he?"

Barry remained silent.

"In fact," continued Lipperstein, "was it really you who locked yourself in?"

"*I think so, yes. I like to be in a quiet place to concentrate before a game. I must have closed the door after Arthur left, locked it, and put the key on the little table.*"

"You see! Even you agree! If the door was locked, the murderer had to come through the window."

"*Not necessarily.*"

The Chief Inspector jumped up.

"How did he enter then?"

"*Obviously, through the door,*" the Ghost replied. "*I'll get back to it and explain, but first, I need a few more details.*"

Lipperstein no longer understood. He sat down and gathered the pages, shuffling them back into one single stack.

"*You told me that you turned the Black Knights around, correct?*" continued Barry.

"Yes, I did. I was surprised to see that Fell had the same habit as you."

"*Which one?*"

"That of turning the Knights around, presumably to make gripping them easier?"

"*I don't do that.*"

"Ah?"

"*Were the White Knights turned around?*"

"Not that I recall, no," answered Lipperstein, frowning.

"*You see. That matches what I just told you.*"

"But..."

"*Yes, Smith told you that I was playing white.*"

"Exactly. He set up the board according to Fell's instructions, making it clear who was playing what." Lipperstein reflected. "Maybe he got them mixed up?"

"*No, he didn't. I was supposed to play black that morning.*"

"Then was it Fell who was mistaken?"

"*Fell? Mistaken? Arthur never makes a mistake, or almost never—even less so when it is a matter of chess. We had been talking about that game since the early hours of the morning, and he was the one who had challenged me, and he positively wanted to play white to show that my opening theories were in error.*"

"So?"

"*So, Arthur was preoccupied by something else.*"

"By what, by Jove?"

"*By my murder!*"

Lipperstein opened his mouth, but no sound came out. Barry had the look of someone who finally understood that he had been deceived—a rare instance—and that that negligence had cost him his life.

"Fell did it?" Lipperstein finally articulated. "But why? And how?"

Barry sat back down. He took the time to prepare his pipe. His gaze was even more disquieting than usual due to his new condition.

"*You read what Featherstone wrote about him, didn't you?*" he asked after having lit his ghostly implement.

"Yes."

"*Where did he live before moving to London a few years ago?*"

Lipperstein looked for the stack of papers on the desk and went through it.

"It says here, in a little village named St Mary Mead."

"*That name doesn't ring a bell?*"

Lipperstein thought a moment. "No, not at all."

"*That's normal, because that village doesn't exist. Featherstone was fooled, just he was by my so-called stamp collecting. But there is another name that resembles it... Think...*"

"I still don't understand," said Lipperstein, confused.

"*What if I said St Mary Bethlehem, as in...*"

"...Bedlam!" the Chief Inspector said, shaking his head.

"Yes! The notorious psychiatric hospital where the criminally insane and other dangerous lunatics are kept."

"But that's where..." Lipperstein started.

Barry, with a wave of his hand, encouraged him to continue.

"Yes. Do you now see how things converge?"

"...That's where Sir Henry Tarford murderous brother, Philip, was imprisoned," finished Lipperstein.

"Exactly, and who might want to kill me more than him?"

Lipperstein passed his hand over his thinning hair.

"But Fell doesn't resemble at all to the Philip Tarford whom I remember."

"Certainly not! After he escaped, he took great care to alter his physical appearance. Try to picture him with shorter hair, several pounds less, and remember his stance..."

"Good Lord! You *are* right!"

"It is obvious that he nursed his desire for revenge during all those years of confinement, looking for a way to make me pay for foiling his plan and getting him arrested. As you recall, Philip is very smart. It took him a long time to plan for this—and I'm sorry to say, he finally succeeded! I bet that if you ask Bedlam, they'll tell you that he studied chess for months before he escaped."

"All that to eventually join your club?"

"Yes—to be near me, to make me like him, until he could deliver that fatal blow. Do you understand now? Philip spent years posing as Arthur Fell only to gain my trust."

"But how did he do it?"

Barry placed his ghostly pipe on the desk.

"*Philip needed to be sure that he and I would be alone. That's why he set up the idea of a challenge. He knew that we would be alone in one of the private rooms on the first floor. That was the perfect place. He knew that one of the* Bishops *would take care of setting it up. Once we were alone, he waited until Smith brought us tea, and then he drugged my cup.*"

"How?"

"*I suppose that the drug was in the same flask that was supposed to contain his medication. If you look into Fell's medical history, I am convinced that you will find that he had no history of illness, despite what Feather-stone believed.*"

"That was part of his plan?"

"*Yes. He wanted everything to seem normal. If he was seen with a flask, he had to have a good explanation for it, hence his so-called chronic malady.*"

Barry picked up his pipe again, and played with it between his fingers.

"*He took advantage of a second when I turned my head. He then poured the drug into my cup. Once he was certain that I had drunk the tea, he left. He was careful to leave the room before the drug took effect. His plan depended on his ability to estimate the lapse of time that would occur next, but he was counting on my habits to the scene accurately for what was to come.*"

"To set the scene?"

"*Yes. I had to be found in a certain position for the illusion to be perfect. He could then finish his dastardly work.*" Barry relit the ghostly fire in his pipe. "*After he had left the room, I locked the door with the key, which I then placed next to me on the little table, before sitting down in the armchair. Then, the drug began to do its work. I fell into a deep sleep. Philip had nothing more to*

131

do but wait and time his next move accurately—which he did. After knocked at the door, he asked for the assistance of a Bishop *who could then testify to the fact that the door was indeed locked from the inside. Do you remember where Smith was standing? Once the door had been broken, Fell entered the room first and rushed toward me—Smith stayed behind. It was enough for Fell to simulate horror upon discovering my corpse—even though, at that point, I was still only asleep!—and ask for the young man to go and get the police..."*

Lipperstein remained mute.

"Then, Philip took out a long blade that he had undoubtedly hidden inside his suit and stabbed me. Just once, right to the heart. My relaxed posture and the small small amount of blood are explained by the fact that I was asleep when I was killed, and therefore my cardiac beats were at a minimum. Once his crime was done, he just had to wait for the arrival of others and fake being upset. Later, he spread out the dirt under the window—although I'm inclined to think he might have done this the day before—to cover his tracks and divert attention."

Barry looked directly into the eyes of the Chief Yard Inspector.

"The rest are details that you can clear by yourself."

Lipperstein cleared his throat. "Indeed."

"You know what my greatest regret in this affair is, Chief Inspector?"

The Chief Inspector nodded negatively.

"It's that, as intelligent as I am, I didn't succeed in unmasking my killer before he could murder me." He paused. *"What a farce! I, who am supposed to be gifted with superior intelligence and vast deductive powers,*

was deceived by a man whom I had met before, and yet succeeded in deceiving me for a number of years."

Lipperstein stood up and prepared to leave. He knew that the next day would be difficult. Barrison watched him while he was getting his things together. The Chief Inspector paused for a moment just as he was about to leave the room.

"Do you know what all this means, Barry?"

"No, what?"

"That you were human."

He said good-bye to the Ghost with a nod of his head.

"We will see each other again, Barry?"

The Ghost smiled at him.

"As often as you wish. You know where to find me."

Lipperstein smiled back.

"So long, then."

And, without a word, he left the room, leaving the Ghost Detective to his somber thoughts.

BARRY BARRISON, GHOST DETECTIVE

THE JEWELS OF THE THAMES

BY CLAUDIO TIZIANO FUSI & LUCIANO BERNASCONI

THE MOON WAS REFLECTED IN THE CALM WATERS OF THE THAMES. THE TWO LOVERS WALKED ALONG THE QUAYS, ARM IN ARM...

IT WAS A GENTLE NIGHT...

The Jewels of the Thames[5]

1.

It was a gentle night; the moon was reflected in the calm waters of the Thames. The two lovers walked along the quays, arm in arm. The evening had begun with a most agreeable dinner, and the two uni students had decided to walk back to their small apartment, taking advantage of the beginning of the warm weather. That was rare enough in London. Terry Edwards and Angela Lake had taken a break from their studies to take full advantage of it. The year was coming to its end, and soon they would have nothing but their exams to worry about.

The day before, Terry had surprised his girlfriend by telling her that he was taking her to a little French restaurant that had opened a few weeks earlier in one of the fashionable sections of London. The buzz about it was good and the conviviality of the place had garnered much critical praise in *Time Out*. The wait was long and the restaurant rather expensive, but the student hadn't hesitated a second. Angela, pragmatic, had at first refused, arguing that she preferred that Terry keep his money rather than spend it on a meal in a posh restaurant, but faced with the disappointed look of her companion and his insistence, she had finally agreed. Terry had argued *carpe diem* with a charming smile.

---

[5] *The Jewels of the Thames* is an expanded variant version of the first *Barry Barrison, Ghost Detective* comic-book story.

The two young people stopped and sat down on a bench. They didn't say a word, content to be in one another's presence. The meal had been excellent, as had the wine.

"When we're married, we'll live in the country," said Terry.

Angela burst out laughing.

"Do you decide that for me without consulting me first? But tell me, are you so sure of my feelings, my dear Terry!"

The young man's face flushed.

"But, I thought that..." he stammered.

Angela's smile became broader. She placed her hand on her companion's arm.

"I'm teasing you, but don't you think it's a bit early to talk of buying a house? Let's finish our studies first, and then we will see."

She placed a kiss on the young man's cheek.

"Let's go home. I'm beginning to feel tired. All that wine has gone to my head and I would like to lie down."

Terry stood up and offered his arm to his girlfriend. They continued their walk for a while along the quiet banks of the Thames before reaching a narrow alley that would take them back toward the heart of the City.

Suddenly, behind them, they heard the screeching of tires and car doors being slammed. Several swear words followed. The couple stopped.

"Did you hear that?" Angela asked.

"Yes. What do you think that was?"

"I have no idea."

The noise intensified. Angela let loose of Terry's arm and walked back down the street to the corner. Slowing, she leaned against the wall and risked a look. Terry cursing her impetuosity approached in his turn.

A gray sedan was parked along the quay. Two men were standing in front of the closed trunk. A dull repeated sound came from it, punctuating their animated discussion. The distance kept the two students from understanding what was going on, but there was no doubt that those two men were not there for some night fishing.

"There is someone inside that trunk, Terry!"

Angela turned toward her boyfriend. Surprised to find him so close, she stifled a cry of surprise.

"Idiot!" she continued, giving him a tap on the arm. "You scared me!"

"I wasn't going to remain standing! Are you certain there is someone in the trunk?"

"Are you deaf? Listen to the noise."

Terry agreed that there was someone in the trunk, and added:

"Let's find a phone box and call 9-9-9. It's the job of the police to take care of these kinds of things."

He grabbed his companion's arm, pulling her back. Angela turned around after having thrown a last glance at the car and the two strange men. They turned around and Angela started searching her purse for some coins while Terry was looking for a red phone box, when they heard a cry.

"*Help!*"

The woman's cry tore through the night. Angela dropped the coins that she had just found. Terry stepped in front of her and went back to the corner.

"*Help!*"

A second cry, mingled with tears, fear, rage and frustration, resounded in their ears. Terry risked a look: the two men had opened the trunk of their car and were now carrying a human form bundled inside a thick carpet. The woman—because it was without a doubt a woman who was shouting—was resisting with all her strength, making her assailants go to great effort not to drop her.

"Come on!" said the man who was holding her by her feet. "We've got to get rid of her as fast as possible!"

He gestured with his head to indicate the edge of the quay.

"Terry, we've got do something!" whispered Angela, clutching the right arm of her companion so hard that her fingers turned white. "There's no time to find a phone box now."

"To do what? I am not like Mark, I don't do karate! Should I go up to them and challenge them to a quiz on Welsh history?"

"Idiot!"

"OK! You win!"

Terry placed a fast kiss on Angela's forehead, and before she had time to react, rushed towards the two men.

"Hank! behind you!" shouted the man who was holding the end of the carpet where the girl's head was.

The other man turned around and saw the young student running towards him.

"Quick!" he ordered his accomplice. "To the river!"

With a quick gesture, he took out a gun from the pocket of his high-collar coat and pointed it toward Terry. Then, without taking the time to aim, he fired twice. The shots resounded in the calm of the London night, tearing the silence like two whip lashes. Angela cried out. Terry had just enough time to shift his balance on his left leg and dive, hitting a wooden crate that broke on impact. A little groggy, he tried to stand up. He felt a sharp pain in his shoulder.

Meanwhile, the two men had taken advantage of that short pause to approach the edge of the quay and, with a sweeping gesture, get rid of their burden by throwing it into the water. The unfortunate woman inside the carpet let out a cry of terror, which quickly turned to gargling as her head went under. She sank inexorably into the icy depths of the Thames. Angela, panicked, saw Terry try to stand up.

"Come on, let's go!" said one man.

The other man—the one named Hank—got behind the steering wheel. The first man walked over to Terry, who clumsily adopted a posture of self-defense, borrowed from what he remembered having seen their friend Mark do during his karate sessions.

The man stopped a few feet away. "If I see you again, you'll end up like her, understood?" he said in a threatening tone.

Terry frowned, trying in vain to get a good picture of his aggressor, but between the darkness and his horrible headache, he could barely see a few indistinct features. The man returned to the car and slammed the door. The tires squealed and the vehicle sped off, leaving a strong odor of burned rubber in its wake.

Angela came out of her hiding place and ran toward her boyfriend.

"Quick! Rescue the girl!" shouted Terry. "I'm all right!"

Angela didn't hesitate. She took off her jacket and plunged into the cold, dark waters of the Thames. Still shivering, Terry walked to the edge of the quay. His vision had cleared, and the pounding of his heart slowed down. His shoulder still hurt, but the pain was endurable. He was happy that neither of the two shots had hit their marks.

Some concentric circles and air bubbles suddenly split the surface of the river. The young man decided to dive. He knew that Angela was a good swimmer, but there was a huge difference between swimming laps in a pool, and diving into icy dark waters looking for a body.

After a first moment of panic, he forced himself to stay calm. He could see almost nothing. Only a halo of pale light coming from a street lamp a few yards away broke the stifling obscurity. He searched right and left, but in vain. He came up for the third time, catching his breath. He was becoming worried.

"Angela!" he shouted.

Only the clapping of the water answered him. He took a deep breath, filling his lungs with the maximum air they could hold, and dived again. He went down deeper. He searched everywhere, without success. Some dirty algae brushed against his face. He as beginning to run out of air... He was about to return to the surface, when a woman's hand suddenly gripped his leg. He easily recognized Angela's. The young woman, nearly out of air too, was clinging to him like a life preserver.

Terry half-saw her face, which showed exhaustion. Forgetting the compression of his lungs, he grabbed Angela's wrist and pulled her up with all his strength. The pain in his shoulder, combined with the lack of air, became almost intolerable.

The fear of death suddenly gave him a last burst of energy. They would not die in those dirty waters! Rage made him forget everything else. He flexed his muscles and pulled again. Below him, air bubbles were starting to escape from Angela's mouth. Panic could be seen in her eyes.

Finally, after a last effort, which almost yanked his arm out of his shoulder, Terry broke through the surface of the water, taking in a new breath with a groan of pain.

Angela emerged right behind him—the very last effort she could have managed. Terry stepped onto the quay, took her under her arms and pulled her up. He then noticed that with her other arm, Angela was gripping the ropes that bound the body of another woman.

Thanks to his good shoulder, he miraculously managed to bring them both out of the icy waters. The carpet, gorged with water, was still wrapped around the other girl's feet, but began floating away on the calm surface of the river.

Angela coughed, spitting out the water in her lungs. She sputtered more than she breathed. The other woman was still unconscious—but alive. Terry and Angela had selflessly risked their own lives to save her. But who was she—and who had wanted her dead?

2.

The two young people were sitting exhausted on the edge of the quay. Their eyes haggard, trying to catch their breath, they remained silent for a while. Angela was the first to regain control of herself. She stood up with difficulty and dragged herself over to the still motionless body of the girl whom they had pulled out of the river. There was a gag over her moth, made of sticky tape. It might have saved her life. She tried to remove it with her hand, but couldn't. She rummaged in her coat looking for some object with which to cut it, and the ropes, but in vain.

She turned toward Terry, who had managed to get up with some difficulty.

"Terry!" she shouted. "We have to find some way for her to get some air into her lungs, otherwise, she'll die!"

The shout woke up the young man. He was shivering with cold and the pain in his shoulder was horrible, but he foraged in the pockets of his jeans and found out a little penknife. He opened the blade with a trembling hand and held it out to his girlfriend.

"You do it," he said while his teeth were chattering. "I'm trembling too much; I might hurt her."

Angela seized the knife and placed the blade next to the girl's mouth. After taking a short breath, she plunged the blade in and sliced the tape open. Angela glanced at Terry, who agreed with a hoarse cough.

"Go ahead!" he said.

The young woman slid her fingers as delicately as possible into the narrow opening and finally managed to tear apart some of the tape. Then she placed her own mouth on the opening, seized the girl's nose, and frantically began mouth-to-mouth resuscitation, drawing on her memories, alternating a good rhythm to send air into the girl's lungs and applying cardiac massages: *one, two, three,* then three expirations of air into the lungs. But perhaps, she was exerting herself for nothing? She thought. She hadn't even taken the time to feel for a pulse...

"Don't stop!" said Terry. "She's coming to!"

The young man picked up the knife that Angela had dropped. With it, he began to cut the ropes that bound the unconscious young woman.

The hands, slim and delicate, of the intended murder victim, appeared. They were freezing. Instinctively, the young man picked them up and squeezed them.

The body made a sudden movement. Then, another jerk. Water ran out of her nose and mouth. A suffocating cough followed, then a halting respiration.

"Terry! She's alive!" said Angela, exhilarated.

The young man dropped the hands that he was trying to warm up and looked at the unfortunate woman who was trying to breathe. The young woman opened her eyes, and slightly shook her locks of red hair.

"Everything is all right now," said Terry. "Your attackers have left. We are friends. You have nothing to fear."

The girl opened her eyes wide. She was haggard, not seeming to know what had happened to her, or where she was. Angela tried to calm her.

"You are on the banks of the Thames," the young student said. "We rescued you after some men threw you into the river. There is no one here except my boyfriend Terry. I'm Angela. You have nothing to fear from us."

It was obvious that the young woman was in a state of shock. Her eyes were rolling in their orbits and her respiration remained very irregular. She was in a state of panic and Angela didn't know what else to do to calm her. Suddenly, the red-haired girl had a fit. Her eyes rolled back in her head and she became still.

"Terry? What's happening?" asked Angela.

The young man placed his fingers on the neck of the woman. "She fainted, I think." He replied. "Let's take her back to our place. In any case, nothing more can be achieved by staying here. Let's go to where we'll be safe and can decide what to do next."

"Why don't we just call the police?"

"What if, before they arrive, these two men return? They're armed. I'm in no state to fight, and neither are you. What will we do then? No, I think it's safer to go home."

He glanced at the girl's inert body, passed his arms under her, and with great effort—one that he no longer thought himself capable off—lifted her. Silently, to save his breath, he started again in the direction of the alley. Angela followed him after having picked up their things.

Half an hour later, the two young people had returned to their apartment in Candlewick. They took the side streets in order to avoid the two would-be killers who might still be in the neighborhood. Terry gently deposited the still unconscious young woman on the couch in the living room of their flat. They then sat in front of her, exhausted.

"What should we do now?" Angela asked.

Terry tried to analyze the situation as calmly as he could.

"I'm not sure. If we call the police, we're going to be barraged with questions, the answers of which we don't have. Plus, she might be in some kind of trouble with the Law."

"But what else can we do? I suppose we should wait until she wakes up and ask her?"

"I don't know, Angela," Terry replied. "This is just as much new to me as it is for you."

"What if we called Mark?"

Terry turned towards his girlfriend. "Why?" he asked.

"He's our friend. Maybe he would have an idea, don't you think so?"

Terry shrugged.

"If you want my honest answer, I think the only thing Mark Tarford cares about is Mark Tarford."

Angela looked angrily at her boyfriend.

"That's not true! I know that you don't much care for him, but you must admit that he's very resourceful."

"OK, OK! Call him. I suppose it can't do any harm."

Angela got up, picked up her phone, and dialed a number.

Terry took advantage of her brief conversation to reexamine what had happened. They had rescued an unknown woman at the risk of their own lives. The two men had tried to kill her. They had no particular accent, were both wearing the same kind of ordinary clothes, making them difficult to identify. Also, they were armed, which proved that they were professionals. Who was their intended victim? Where did she come from?

Angela hung up. "Mark is on his way," she said.

"What did he say?"

"He said we did the right thing."

Terry smiled sarcastically. "That's nice of him."

"Stop it, will you? We have other fish to fry!"

The young man got up and walked to the kitchen.

"You're right. Sorry! I'll make us some coffee while we wait for him."

Angela smiled. She was not unaware of the fact that Terry had always been a little jealous of Mark Tarford. She had dated Mark a few times in the past, but that was several years ago. However, Terry couldn't keep himself from bringing it up when he felt angry.

Terry and Angela's relationship was solid now, and Mark had remained a good friend to both of them, but Terry still hated having to depend on the one who had been his girlfriend's first flame. He had honestly admitted to Angela that it was a question of male ego. Even if the young woman understood what her companion might feel, it was still necessary in this case to consider their options. If they didn't want to go to the authorities, Mark Tarford seemed to be the only one able to help.

Fifteen minutes later, the elegant young man knocked at the door. Swallowing his male pride, Terry greeted him with a friendly handshake. He invited Mark in and offered him a cup of coffee; Mark took it after having hung his expensive coat on the rack. The three students then moved to the kitchen. Angela gave Mark a rapid account of the night's events. As the story went on, Mark's expression became shocked, amazed at the risks taken by his friends. The young woman finally ended her story, placing her empty coffee cup on the table.

"So, what do you think?" she asked.

Mark took a deep breath. "I think you've been quite reckless, but in all honesty, I think I would have acted just the same in similar circumstances." He looked admiringly at Terry. "And as for you, my friend, bravo!"

Terry was surprised. "Why?"

"I probably wouldn't have had the balls to act as you did," admitted Mark

"I didn't have a choice, to tell the truth," Terry replied. "If we hadn't acted, there's no doubt that that young woman would have died."

"Yes, but if that thug had been a better shot, you would be lying on the quays of the Thames with a bullet in your body right now."

Terry shrugged, causing him some pain in his shoulder. "Neither of the two shots hit me, but I hurt my shoulder when I fell, and it's still quite painful."

"We were very lucky," Angela said, shivering. "Thinking about it, it was pure folly."

"I don't think you should remain here this weekend just in case," Mark said, breaking the silence. "My folks are gone on a business trip until the middle of next week. I suggest then that you come and spend the week-end with me at the Manor—with your mystery guest, of course. Maybe we can figure out a way to find out what really happened. What do you say?"

"I don't know," Angela answered. "Terry? Do you think that's a good idea?"

The young man thought about it. Mark's idea was tempting. Their flat was small and there was no room in it for the mystery woman outside of the living room couch. Also, he was concerned that their aggressors might have tracked them down. He suspected that this affair was quite out of the ordinary and might have far reaching consequences.

"In agree. Thank you, Mark. We will join you there as soon as our survivor regains consciousness."

"Bad idea, my friend. We should leave immediately. The sooner you are safe, the better it is. I have a big car. We can carry that young woman, even unconscious, without any difficulties."

"He's right, Terry," said Angela. "I don't feel safe here..."

Terry passed his hand through his girlfriend's hair, then turned to Mark and said:

"OK! Let's go!"

3.

Tarford Manor was the ancestral dwelling of the Tarford family. Its founder, Sir William Tarford, had had it built right after the great fire that had ravaged London in 1666. The fire had destroyed thousands of buildings, sparing no neighborhood, even the richest ones. Sir William, who had amassed quite a nest egg by trading with the Continent, was impressed by the unusual character of a house that had resisted the flames for hours. After the fire was brought under control, he had made an offer to buy it, and its owner, only too happy to get rid of a property that he thought no longer worth much, and wanting to leave that city as fast as possible, had agreed to sell it for a very reasonable price.

For years afterward, Sir William had restored and rebuilt the house to make into the dwelling that he had always dreamed of. The restored manor had become a model for the area, and Sir William something of a celebrity. At his death in 1697, his son, Sir James Tarford, had continued his work. The neighborhood had eventually been rebuilt and became one of the most fashionable in all of London. Alas, in 1771, bad investments forced Sir William's grandson, Sir Arthur Tarford, to part with it. The Manor then passed from hand to hand for many years, becoming the home of bankers, merchants, and even one reformed freebooter. It was only in the 19th century that Sir Henry Tarford had bought it back. He lived there until his death; the dwelling was then occupied by one of Sir Henry's friends, Barry Barrison, until his murder in very strange circumstances.

Sir Henry's solicitors eventually managed to track down a distant cousin from the branch of the Tarford family that had emigrated to the New World in the mid-1800s. But they had expressed little interest in relocating to England and the building had fallen into relative abandon, until the Wall Street crash of 1929. The financial crisis had forced Mark's grandfather, Quincy Tarford, to leave the United States and to go back to England. That proud and upright man, who had been wounded during the Great War, was lucky enough to reclaim a portion of the family fortune in Europe, and restore a property that he had always known was his family's legacy. When his wife had passed away, Sir Quincy had made his elder son promise that the Manor would forever remain in the Tarford family.

Today it was Mark's parents, John and Julia, who owned it and lived there, even though their business often took them abroad. Nevertheless, the young man knew how important the Manor was to his family and understood that one day, he would inherit it.

Mark parked his car in the street, a few yards from the wrought iron gate. He got out of the vehicle without shutting off the motor. Terry got out from the passenger's side and joined his friend, who had already opened the rear door. Angela had also gotten out. The two men carefully lifted the young woman, who was still unconscious, and, preceded by Angela, went down the little stone path that led to the entrance of the manor.

"Be careful of the sixth step," whispered Mark, "it's still broken."

A few minutes later, the young woman had been stretched out on a bed in a guest room, and the three friends were chatting in the grand salon near the fireplace.

"Let's wait to see if our survivor wakes up by herself," said Mark. "I'll take the first watch. You two, go and lie down in the blue bedroom. I'll you if she wakes up. We'll talk then."

"I don't think I can sleep," Terry replied. "I'm still too tense—and too sore."

"Me neither. I don't want to go lie down, Mark," added Angela. "I'm too worried about her. Should we call a doctor?"

"And tell him what?" Mark said. "That you saved someone from being drowned in the Thames? He'd want to call the police. No, we have no other choice but to wait until she wakes up. I felt her pulse; it's strong. She is breathing normally; she doesn't have a fever. And I threw several blankets over her so that she won't get cold."

"What about the risks of hypothermia," Terry cut in.

"That's what the blankets are for," Mark replied, annoyed. "Once again, I think we should wait until she wakes up."

A sarcastic reply came to Terry's mind, but Angela put her hand on his arm and the young man relaxed.

"Sorry, Mark, I'm just in a foul mood."

"No problem, pal. I understand. Then you both relax here in front of the TV while I'll keep an eye on our Jane Doe."

And without waiting for a response, Mark Tarford left.

Terry was trying to hang on as hard as he could to the slippery stones of the quay. As soon as he tried to pull himself up, he felt himself being pulled down again by some kind of supernatural force. He panicked. His shoulder was painful, and each move he made threatened to tear him apart. His breath was short; he had exhausted his last resources. He was going to die—to drown like a rat! With the strength of despair, he began to swim with all his strength, with a single objective in mind: to reach the edge of the quay; it was only one or two strokes away. But once again, he felt himself pulled down and saw his salvation move even further away.

He opened his mouth to shout, to cry for help, but water flowed into his lungs. In a last effort, he tried to move forward. But the accursed force pulled him down again, toward the dark depths of the river....

"Terry! Wake up!"

Mark Tarford was trying to wake up his friend, who was curled up on the couch, sleeping in a fetal position. He had been shaking him for several minutes without success. He could not pull him out of his nightmare.

On a neighboring couch, Angela also was resting, exhausted by the events of the night, her knees pulled up, her head over a cushion.

"Terry! Wake up!" shouted Mark.

The young student awoke with a start. He gasped for air as if he were indeed about to drown. Then he stifled a cry of surprise and straightened up. His face was covered in sweat.

"Well, pal, you were having the daddy of all nightmares, it seems?" said Mark.

"You're right," sighed Terry, glad to be out of it.

"Come! The girl is awake."

He gave Angela a gentle tap on her shoulder, that brought out a groan.

"Sorry, I just fell asleep," she murmured.

"No problem," said Terry. "Let's go."

He stood up, making his painful joints crack, and they both followed Mark upstairs toward the guest bedroom.

The young woman had opened her eyes and was looking absently at the ceiling. Her long red curls formed a big mass on either side of her face. She was pale, and her features were drawn by fear and fatigue.

When Mark, Terry and Angela entered the room, she smiled at them timidly. The three young students approached the bed and each sat down on a chair.

"Good evening, Miss," Mark began with a smile that he wanted to be as reassuring as possible.

"Good evening," she replied in a low and tired voice.

"You are safe here, "here" being my home, Tarford Manor in Kensington. I'm Mark Tarford and these two are Terry Edwards and Angela Lake. It's thanks to them that you didn't end up at the bottom of the Thames."

The red head girl shook her head.

"I vaguely remember," she replied, after having cleared her throat. "Thank you, both."

"You're very welcome," Terry said with a wink.

The young woman smiled back.

"Could you tell us your name?" asked Mark. "Also, what happened to you? Why was someone—two someones, in fact—trying to kill you?"

The young woman sat up on the bed. Terry got up to place another pillow under her back, so as to make her as comfortable as possible.

"My name is Maureen Thompson," she began, after taking a deep breath. "I live in Ingersham, a little village between London and Oxford. For a few months now, I have been managing an antique shop."

"So how did you find yourself rolled up like a sausage in an old rug ready to be thrown to the bottom of the Thames?" asked Mark.

"Mark! Could you phrase the question differently?" Terry asked indignantly. "That's a little rough!"

"Don't worry, Terry, that's not important," Maureen said with a sad smile. "It may be a little brutal, but compared to what I have lived through, that's nothing." She shivered, but got control of herself quickly. "I will tell you that I don't understand anymore than you do how I came to this. Two men came into my shop at the beginning of the afternoon. They wanted information on some jewel that I supposedly picked up on a trip to Brazil a few months ago. But I never went to Brazil! I could never afford such a long trip, and probably couldn't endure being cooped up for so long in an airplane."

She interrupted herself, getting a little more comfortable. Her green eyes were now sparkling, and her cheeks, while still pale, had taken on a little color.

"What happened next?" Terry inquired.

"The two men insisted. They wanted to take a look at the rarest pieces in our inventory. Suspicious, I only showed them some items of little value. I wanted to know whom I was dealing with."

A smile appeared on Mark's face. He found Maureen delightful. It took good presence of mind to react as she had done.

"So what happened?" he asked.

"Well, they didn't know anything about antiques," the young woman replied, relaxing a little. "I showed them a terracotta pot made by my nine year-old nephew, telling them that it came from a dig in Africa, and that it dated back to the twelfth century…"

That time, Mark couldn't hold back a laugh.

"How did they react?"

"They nodded approvingly! One of them even took down notes! He asked for its price. I told him that such an object was priceless, and that its value was more historical than financial. However, I told them that I had been contacted by the Louvre in Paris, and the British Museum, and that one had offered me 25,000 pounds for it."

153

"Wasn't it risky to make such a statement?" asked Terry. "That might have motivated them to steal it."

"You're right," replied Maureen, "but I didn't think about it at the time. I only wanted to be sure that I was dealing with people who were what they pretended to be. I had thought I was only telling them the most improbable lie that came into my mind."

"Then what happened?" asked Mark, more and more admiring.

"They left, excusing themselves for having bothered me."

"Is that all?"

The young woman pulled her knees up, now less at ease.

"Yes, that's what I believed. The rest of the afternoon went as usual. I must say, Ingersham has become a little strange these last few months. People seem to hesitate to leave their houses, and it is at night that they come out. I took advantage of the remainder of the day to finish some inventory that I had started." She interrupted herself to turn toward Mark. "May I please have a glass of water?"

"Yes, of course," replied the young student. He got up, saying, "I will be back," and left the room.

Terry moved about on his chair, smiling at Angela and Maureen.

"I can never thank you both enough," the red-haired girl said after a few seconds. "Without you, I know that I would have died."

"You're welcome." replied Terry, little used to that kind of compliment. "But Angela was the first to dive in after you."

"You must be very brave," said Maureen.

"I had no time to think, honestly," replied Angela.

Mark returned with a big glass of water. Maureen drank it all quickly, thanking him with a nod of the head; then she began her story again.

"I close at eight. All my inventory was done, and except for those two strange visitors, no one else had come into the shop. As usual, I closed the store in the front and I left through the back, where I park my car." She held back a shiver. "I didn't see or hear anything. I only felt that someone had put a wet piece of cloth with an intoxicating odor over my face. Then, nothing. I passed out."

Maureen was trembling at the remembrance of these sinister events. She drew the blankets up to cover her knees, as if their presence could mask the violent emotions that she felt. Mark came to sit next to her on the edge of the bed.

"Do you want to take a break?"

"No, it will be all right," Maureen said after a while, with a feeble smile. "In any event what followed is very confusing. I recovered consciousness in the dark. I was in a small, enclosed space and I heard the sound of a motor. There were whispered discussions of which I understood almost nothing..."

She nervously touched a little pendant shaped like an insect which hung on a silver chain around her neck.

"I realized I was in the boot of a car. I supposed that it was the same men of had come during in the afternoon who had returned and kidnapped me. Then..."

She interrupted herself again, without having the strength to continue. Angela got up and put a comforting hand on her shoulder.

"What followed, we know, Maureen. It's not worth the trouble to tell it to us. Get some rest until tomorrow. Then we will decide what to do next."

Mark stood up in his turn.

"Angela is right," he said. "Stay and rest as long as you desire. There's no urgency." He looked at his watch. "It's four o'clock in the morning. I think that all of us would profit by getting some sleep."

Terry joined Angela.

"Use the bedroom across the hall," continued Mark. "Me, I'll grab some winks here in an armchair in order to be sure that Maureen is all right."

The young woman opened her mouth to protest.

"Don't tell me I can't do that," Mark continued with a smile before she had time to say anything. "I don't want say that the Tarfords don't know how to take care of their guests."

Maureen agreed without saying a word. She, in fact, felt relieved to not be alone in this new place. Worn out, she put her head on the pillow, closed her eyes, and fell asleep immediately.

Terry and Angela left the room silently, leaving Mark to watch over the young woman.

When Terry lay down beside his girlfriend and closed his eyes, he felt that there was something that bothered him about Maureen's story, but he didn't know what. He was hoping that several hours of sleep would help him figure it out.

4.

It was the odor of warm coffee that brought Angela out of her sleep. The young woman stirred. She felt stiff from after having slept anywhere but in her own bed. She had recovered her strength. She looked around the room. The morning sun was entering through the windows with a bright and refreshing light. Everything seemed so calm at Tarford Manor that the events of the night before seemed almost unreal.

The empty spot beside her still bore the imprint of her boyfriend's body. The door leading to the corridor was open, and she heard a discussion coming from the salon below. When she joined the two young men, they were already in the middle of a discussion with cups of hot coffee in front of them. Terry stood up to greet his girlfriend and bring her a cup of coffee.

"I knew that I had seen her face before," he said.

Mark was in the process of leafing through a bunch of scientific journals. A satisfied smile on his lips, he found what he'd been looking for and showed it to his friends.

"But that's Maureen!" exclaimed Angela.

"Yes," Mark replied, "except that she told us that her name was Thompson, but she is, in fact, Maureen *Simpson,* a medium who's part of some kind of advanced parapsychological experimental study group at Oxford."

Terry and Angela looked at the magazine. There was no doubt: it really was the same woman. The article was a little over two years-old, but the photo didn't allow for any doubt.

"Why do you think she lied to us about her name?" asked Angela.

"Maybe she was afraid?" replied Terry.

"Afraid of what?" asked Angela.

"Of us, of course!" said Terry.

"Of us?" Angela stared at her companion, almost incredulous.

"Why is that so strange? Do you trust unknown people right off the bat?" said Terry.

"But we're the ones who saved her life!" replied Angela.

"Yes, but maybe she thinks we could be from a rival group trying to get the same thing out of her than those other men did," said Terry. "It's not impossible after all that she went through last night."

Mark stepped in:

"She is likely panicked and in a state of confusion. I don't find abnormal that she would try to protect herself by giving us a false name."

"Do we know that she didn't try to flee during the night while we were all asleep?" asked Angela. "That's what I would have done."

Mark burst out laughing. "You women are a lot more wily than we men! But no, I can assure you that Maureen hasn't run away. I went to check on her a half-hour ago and she was still asleep."

"But she still lied to us," Terry interjected, "even if it was for a good reason."

"True," Angela said, munching on a croissant. "That's why it's up to us to gain her confidence and to act so that she stops being afraid of us, but sees us as friends."

"How do we do that?" said Terry. "We have exams coming up. We can't spend weeks with her to win her over."

Mark looked at his two friends with a conspiratorial expression on his face. "I have an idea," he began, "but you're going to think it's stupid..."

"I've known you for ten years, Mark, so nothing from you could surprise me anymore," said Angela.

Terry slapped his friend on the shoulder. "Go ahead. I'm curious to see what you have in mind!"

Mark straightened up on his chair.

"After Sir Henry Tarford passed away, in the late 1890s, one of the residents of Tarford Manor was a remarkable man, an aristocrat who was supremely intelligent and had developed great deductive powers. He was an amateur sleuth who often collaborated with Scotland Yard and solved many complex cases that totally baffled the police."

Angela frowned. "You mean, someone like Sherlock Holmes, Solar Pons or Sexton Blake?"

"Yes, someone just like that, but not as well known. His name was Sir Barry Barrison. I believed he died in the early 1900s. He was murdered by one of his peers in a chess club in some strange circumstances. I found his name on some old papers that my parents stored in the attic, and then I did some research in the local archives, and...."

"That's all very interesting, but how is it relevant?" interrupted Terry. "I'm sure that if any of us had his set of skills, we could easily solve Maureen's mystery, but we can't very well call on a dead man to do it in our place."

Mark cleared his throat. "I was coming to the strangest part of the story. As I said, Barrison was murmured but..." Here, he made a theatrical pause, then continued in a deep voice. "...His ghost, legend has it, still resides within the walls of Tarford Manor."

Terry burst out laughing.

"Ah, this time, you've really lost your grip, Mark! You now believe in ghosts?"

Angela, who had had been listening while perusing the contents of the article about Maureen, interjected:

"I think I see where you're going," she said in a serious tone. "You think that Maureen, who is a psychic, may be able to contact this Barry Barrison ghost in order for him to help us—and in the process come to trust us and create a bond with us?"

Mark agreed in silence. Terry looked at each of his two friends, one after the other, incredulous.

"You are both serious, aren't you? Angela darling, you can't be believing in ghosts!"

Faced with their silence, Terry concluded that his friends did. He stood up and began to walk up and down the kitchen.

"My word!" he said. "You're both mad as a hatter! We're students with a solid scientific background. We are rational. And now, you propose to use a so-called psychic to talk to the ghost of a second-rate Sherlock Holmes who died almost a century ago? Should we also call on the ghosts of Lone Bardo and John Mist? With them, we could play poker all night."

Angela got up and went over to Terry.

"Listen, I know that seems crazy, but what do we risk? I never much believed in ghost stories, but if that helps Maureen to trust us and let us figured out what really happened last night, why not give it a try?"

Terry stared at his girlfriend. He knew her to be rational and reasonable. They were at an impasse. They couldn't go to the authorities and Maureen was hiding something from them. He sighed and placed a kiss on Angela's forehead.

"OK then, but will she agree to this?"

"I will."

The three friends turned at once toward the door. Standing on the threshold, a blanket on her shoulders, her flaming red hair framing her pretty face, Maureen Simpson was looking at them with a shy smile.

"I overheard the end of your conversations," she said apologetically. "If you think that summoning the shade of this Barry Barrison can help find out what happened to me, you can count on me."

5.

"So you were spying on us?" said Terry.

The young woman came into the room. Mark brought forward a chair. Before she had finished sitting down, the young Englishman had put a cup of hot coffee in front of her. She thanked him, took a swallow, and continued:

"I am not an enemy, Terry. All three of you saved my life. I owe you a debt that I can never repay. Get that kind of thought out of your head." She smiled. "Can we start over?" she proposed.

"Of course!" answered Angela, when her two friends didn't say a word. "I'd like that. So you are willing to try to contact that Barry Barrison?"

"Why not?" replied Maureen.

"Will you excuse me," added Terry. "I shouldn't have been as distrustful as I was, but you must admit that I had some good some reasons. Why didn't you give us your real name?"

Maureen shook her head. "I don't know. I guess I panicked. I didn't know who you really were…"

"Let's forget about that," Mark interrupted, "and return to Barry Barrison. Do you think you could contact his spirit, Maureen, summon his ghost?"

"Honestly, I don't know," the red-haired girl replied, after taking a sip of her coffee. "Spiritualism is not an exact science, it's an opening of the mind, based on faith and will, like extra-sensory perception. As you know from that article, I have participated in some para-psychological experimental studies at Oxford, but so far, no solid rules have yet been discovered. They're still groping in the dark with theories about quantum states and other wild notions."

She stopped. Mark, Terry and Angela were listening attentively.

"If there is such a thing as a spirit, a ghost, or an ectoplasmic entity, residing in this house," she continued, "I *might* be able to contact them, but nothing is certain. First, I need to find out about them in order to be able to communicate with them."

"I'll give you everything I dug up about Barry Barrison," said Mark. "Honestly, it isn't much. Do you need it right now?"

"It'll be a start. Have you researched him at the British Library?"

Mark remained silent a moment. "I confess I hadn't even thought about that."

"I can take care of that," Angela said. "Do you need anything specific about him?"

Maureen shook her head. "No," she replied, becoming more animated. "Anything written about him at the time will be useful, even if it's only anecdotes."

Her face was relaxed and her eyes were shining, full of renewed energy.

"How are you going to proceed?" asked Terry. "Everyone will sit in a circle around a table in the dark, touching hands?"

His remark made the young woman smile. "No. Those are clichés dating from the last century. It's not necessary to set such a stage. I only have to be calm, meditate and concentrate on the so-called ghost, and hope that he'll be in a mood to talk."

"In a mood?" Terry repeated, surprised. "Because ghosts have moods?"

"Just like we do," replied Maureen in a serious tone. "If ghosts are the souls of the dead who have gotten stuck here and not been able to move beyond this plane of reality, it is because whatever they are is still reacting to exterior stimuli—whatever happened to them, or around them. So that requires a kind of independent consciousness, and one of the products of consciousness is, for lack of a better term, *mood*."

Maureen saw a look of perplexity of her three friends' faces, so she added, "That's a short way of explaining it. Later, if we have more time, and you are really interested about it, we can talk at some more length and I can tell you about all the theories on the subject. But right now, I don't think we need to worry about it."

"Right!" Mark approved. "Yes, we're a little confused—skeptical even—about what you just told us, but as far as I'm concerned, you wouldn't have been working with these Oxford brains if there weren't some kind of truth behind all of this. We're all in agreement that we need something—or someone—to help us solve this mystery, so why not proceed?"."

"You said you have to be calm and meditate. Do you need anything special?" asked Angela.

"Not really; just a quiet room, a comfortable armchair, and that's it."

"I can set up the regency room," said Mark, standing up. "When do you want to start?"

"As soon as possible, but after I've had the time to read all the documents about Barry Barrison that you're going to give me."

"All right," said Terry. "Angela and I are going to go the British Museum right now. We'll be back this afternoon."

"And I'll dash to the attic to get the papers I found," added Mark.

The three of them prepared to leave the room. Mark stopped when he reached the door.

"Maureen, you're welcome to come with me. You should consider this your own home."

Later in the day, the little group reconvened in the Regency Room of Tarford Manor.

Maureen was studying a stash of papers when Terry and Angela, led by Mark, entered. Tea and biscuits had been set up on a side table.

"I'm so grateful to you two for pulling me out of the river," said Maureen.

"Ah! Anyone would have done the same thing without any second thoughts," said Angela. "It's true that, in retrospect, it was a bit foolhardy, but neither Terry nor I hesitated a second. I dived, and he followed."

Maureen's eyes became a little misty with tears. She understood that she owed her life to these two young people who had decided to risk their own lives to rescue a perfect stranger. Angela, understanding her emotions, went to her and took hugged her.

"Now, Terry and I found some really interesting information about Barry Barrison in the papers of the times," Angela said after a moment, if only to change the topic of conversation. "He was a rather unusual person, it seems," she continued with a smile.

"In what way?" asked Maureen, curious.

"As Mark said, he was intelligent, gifted with an extraordinary analytical mind. I have found information about several criminal cases that he helped solve in collaboration with a Chief Inspector Harvey Lipperstein."

"Do you have any details?"

"Not a lot. There might be more in the Scotland Yard archives that have been declassified and are open to the general public, but we would need to be granted permission to look at them, and that would require more time than we have," she continued, "but after reading all these articles, it's clear Barry Barrison was in good standing with the authorities."

"Did he have a Watson?"

Angela laughed heartedly.

"No, I couldn't find any reference to anyone who might have recorded his cases. That might explain his relative obscurity. It would have been rather useful to us today."

"And no Moriarty either?" asked Maureen.

Angela's good humor was contagious and the young red-haired woman was no longer suffering from melancholy.

"I couldn't find any."

"Mark said he'd been murdered. Do we know by whom?"

"It's not clear," replied Angela with a slight conspiratorial air. "He belonged a chess club and apparently, he was murdered by another member. I couldn't find out more details."

Maureen became serious again. "That's doesn't seem right, does it?"

"Why?"

"Ordinarily, the spirits of the dead haunt the place where they died."

Angela frowned. "I see. You mean that Mark might be mistaken in thinking that Barry Barrison's ghost could be here rather than at that chess club?"

"Yes, but not necessarily. There are a few recorded cases where the ghost is fund haunting another place, but that's rare, and there's usually a good reason for it."

Angela pulled out a sheet of paper.

"The chess club in question was called *The Queen's Pawn*," she said, "and it no longer exists today. It's been turned into a high-rise office building."

Maureen stood up and turned toward Mark who, with Terry's help, had been moving some of the cumbersome furniture. A table that was used for meals, too heavy to be easily moved, had been pushed against a wall, A leather armchair had been placed at an angle in front of the fireplace. The curtains on the windows were drawn, masking the sunlight.

"I must ask Mark where he got the idea that the ghost is haunting Tarford Manor," said Maureen.

Angela stood up in her turn.

"Is it necessary that you should be alone during the séance, or can we stay?" asked Terry.

"On the contrary, you should stay, but you should remain totally quiet and take things seriously."

"Don't worry," Terry replied. "Even if I sometimes give the impression of fooling around, I can stay serious when necessary, and you can trust me."

"Perfect!" replied Maureen. "Now, I need time to prepare myself. Mark, why do you think Barry Barrison is haunting the walls of Tarford Manor as opposed to the place where he was killed?"

The young man shrugged.

"It's rumor I heard my father mention when I was a child, but I have no evidence either way."

"Hmm. I better go and study all the documents you two have gathered. Maybe the answer is somewhere in there."

Mark and Angela gave Maureen a stack of yellowed papers.

"Take your time," said Mark. "We'll wait until you are ready."

Maureen to a corner of the room and began studying the dossier. Terry and Mark took a last look at the room, which would perhaps soon be the scene of a very strange experience.

6.

The afternoon was now drawing to its close. The sun was beginning to decline and the evening coolness descended upon London. In the Regency Room of Tarford Manor, four young people were ready to invoke the spirit of a dead man. For several hours, Mark, Terry, and Angela had been patient while Maureen was learning all she could about Barry Barrison. After a wait that seemed endless, the young medium announced that she was ready.

"We don't have wait for night?" asked Terry.

"No, that's not necessary," Maureen replied. "Judging from what I read, I don't think that our friend Barry is the type to wait until nightfall to show up..." She paused. "In fact, if he is really like he is portrayed, I'm more afraid that nothing can make him manifest himself if he doesn't want to."

"What do you mean?" asked Angela.

Angela was seating on the floor cross-legged.

"I mean that it won't be we who are calling him forth, but he who will decide whether to show himself."

Mark couldn't help shivering.

"I don't understand," he said, shaking his head. "Isn't it the medium who creates a link with the beyond?"

Terry sat down beside his girlfriend; he, too, was a little cold.

"Ah, but there's no normal link here! Barrison wasn't killed here, but at that chess club near the Angel. If his ghost is here, rather than there, it's because he has a good reason for it. He isn't bound to the place in the usual manner."

Mark rubbed his fingers, which felt very cold.

"Then, what do we do? Do we get a cup of tea and just wait until he manifests himself?"

Maureen smiled back and sat down in the armchair.

"No. Let's try."

"*At last!*"

The four young people turned toward the voice that had said uttered words. Angela could not hold back a gasp. As for Terry, he stifled a few swear words. Mark Tarford remained there with his mouth half-opened.

Sitting down cross-legged on the table was the translucent shape of a man about fifty years-old. His smiling face sported an elegant mustache. He wore a deer hunter hat and an open Gabardine coat that revealed a white shirt underneath. He looked at them, one after the other, puffing on an equally translucent pipe that emitted odorless smoke.

"*Excuse me for the sensation of cold you're experiencing,*" he continued, without seeming to notice the shock that his sudden appearance had produced in the group. "*But despite all those years trying to get used to my, er, condition, I still cannot quite control the cold which originates from the place whence I come. Be reas-*

sured, however," he continued smiling, "*it will dissipate after a few minutes.*"

Maureen was the first to be able to speak.

"You are Sir Barry Barrison, aren't you?" she asked, in a not very confidant voice.

"*In the flesh!*" replied the ghost, stepping down agilely from the table. "*If you will pardon my expression.*"

He approached Mark.

"*And this is the current heir of the Tarford line,*" he said, examining the young man from head to toe. "*I am delighted to meet you, Mark. If it were possible, I would shake your hand, but as you realize, that's not to be.*"

He winked. He then looked in the direction of Terry and Angela. He understood who they were instantly.

"*And here's the brave young couple who risked their lives to save a stranger. That's rare, even in my days. I congratulate you, even if you acted somewhat rashly.*"

Then he turned toward Maureen. His sharp eyes became riveted to those of the young woman, who swallowed with difficulty. She had never been present at such an event and didn't know how to react. The ghost seemed to be friendly, but one thing was certain, she had not summoned him, so she knew she would be incapable of banishing him back.

"*And this is the famous Maureen Simpson, the one who has drawn all this attention,*" said Barry, "*the one who is at the center of this mystery, and that clumsy attempted murder!*"

"You already know that?" Angela managed to articulate.

"*Know what?*" asked Barry, without turning around.

"What happened last night."

169

This time the ghost turned his face toward her. His expression was severe.

"*Who do you think I am, young woman?*" he asked in a voice that became cavernous. "*I have been watching you since yesterday.*"

His voice returned to a normal tone. Mark staggered and leaned against the armchair.

"Then, you weren't just a legend…" he murmured.

"*No, young man, I'm not a legend, even if I concede that my activity has slowed down considerably this century. But whose fault is it? Rationalism that claims to explain everything! But enough empty talk! If I am here, it is for a reason. Stop looking at me as if I were a vampire and let's review the facts!*"

Maureen sat up and grabbed Mark's arm. Terry and Angela remained on the floor, relaxing a little. As Barry had claimed, the temperature had returned to normal.

"Where do we begin?" asked Maureen, in an hesitant voice.

"*By explaining why you misled your friends,*" replied the ghost.

"What?"

"*You told them that you have no connection with South America. Yet, that ring on your finger comes from Peru. As far as I can tell, it's authentic; it comes from the region of Machu Picchu and is several centuries old.*"

"But I told you I suffered from vertigo," she stammered. "I can't fly…."

"*Ah! Vertigo! How clumsy,*" Barry continued. "*Vertigo is the product of being connected to the ground under your feet. You cannot suffer from vertigo in one of your flying contraptions, no more than I can have a headache. I suspect that the action of these two men was not a product of chance, was it?"*

He stopped, satisfied with his demonstration. Maureen looked embarrassed. Mark stood up and stood facing her, his arms crossed.

"Is he right?" he asked, in a rather harsh voice.

She nodded, not looking him in the eyes. The young man sighed.

"Why did you lie to us?"

Terry stood up. "I knew that there was something fishy about her story."

"Is there something else that you have lied to us about?" asked Angela, approaching the young woman and placing a hand on her knee.

Her head lowered, weeping, Maureen remained silent.

"She also lied about her business," added Barry. *"Or I should say, one of her businesses."*

"What do you mean?" asked Mark.

He had gotten over his apprehension and was now talking to Barry as if he was a real physical person.

"If you look at her hands, you will be notice some little marks," said the ghost.

"Some reddish stains," Angela confirmed. "That's normal, considering she's ginger."

"That was what I first thought," continued Barry, *"but if you look carefully at her wrists, you will see a regular mark that goes all the way around them."*

"So?" Angela didn't understand what the Barry was getting at.

Maureen was rubbing her wrists as if she wanted to erase the traces that had become too visible.

"Gloves! Thin leather gloves, the kind that you wear while driving—or to not leave fingerprints behind!

171

I think that our Maureen is engaged in another business on top of her little shop selling knickknacks of dubious provenance. You don't have to be a ghost to suppose that the two men who kidnapped her came to get back something that she had stolen from them. Am I wrong, Maureen?"

Maureen finally raised her head. She had stopped crying. Her eyes were red and she felt ashamed. Terry was now standing beside Mark.

"I think that it's time now to tell us the whole truth, Maureen," said Mark. "We can't help you unless you're honest with us."

He pointed at the ghost and added:

"Sir Barry discovered in a few minutes what we couldn't piece together in more than a day. If there's anyone who can get you out of trouble, it's him. But for that, you must tell us everything, OK?"

The young medium stood up, still pouting. Her eyes looked at everyone in the room, then stopped upon the ghost, whom they studied for a long time, with a mixture of respect and anger. Barry stared back at her without blinking, drawing some spectral puffs from his pipe.

"Sit down, it's going to be a long story," she finally said.

7.

Maureen Simpson was aware that she no longer had a choice. She also wondered if it wasn't already too late... But it didn't make any difference; her situation couldn't get any worse. She took a deep breath, and after having stared at her listeners, she began:

"For several years, I was part of an archeological team that went across the world; it was a way of paying for my education. At first, I was only a hired hand, mostly doing the grunt work, and managing the equipment. Eventually, I became interested in those expeditions, and became passionate about all these long-dead civilizations that. That, plus my scientific background, gave me a second string to my bow, as it were..."

She interrupted herself for a moment, her eyes shining, her gaze lost in the distance, recalling certain memories of her past.

"It's fascinating to dig around the past of those civilizations, even if it is only with a tiny brush and not with a pick. You learn about the way of life of these people, their fears, their beliefs, their riches. When I say *riches*," she continued, sensing Mark's disapproval, "I don't mean just their material riches, but everything that made the strength of their cultures..."

"Get to the facts, please," Terry cut in.

The young woman smiled at him sadly, unhappy that the young man thought her so venal.

"A little more than six months ago, I was approached by a small group of people who wanted to go and dig around a particular site in Brazil."

"*Approached where?*" inquired Barry.

"At my regular place of business."

"*Your boutique?*"

"Yes. It was the end of January. Three men came. One of them introduced himself as Professor Vlatov Klost."

"What a strange surname," remarked Angela.

"He's Romanian, from The University of Budapest. He showed me some identification. The other two were his assistants. They spoke little, with a strong accent."

"How did they find out about you?" intervened Terry. "Why go into a little village to search for someone with the kind of qualifications that, I imagine, would be much easier to find in London?"

"*Excellent question, Terry!*" threw in Barry.

The young man smiled. He was beginning to like that ghost.

"That is one of the first questions I asked them," Maureen replied. "Even though I lied about my vertigo, I do not like flying, so I carefully choose the kind of expeditions I agree to join. Professor Klost said me that he had stumbled on an article that I had written a short time before about my last job. He told me that he had very much liked my analysis and felt there was in my writing evidence of a great passion for archeology and its mysteries."

"What was that article about?" asked Mark.

"I wrote it after a short stay in France, near Reims, where I took part in a dig at a Gallo-Roman site. At that time, the city was still known as Durocortorum. I submitted my article to *the Oxford Journal of Archeology* and they printed it. Professor Klost added that he expected to leave soon and he didn't have time to put together a large team. He had enough funding from his university to hire me and his two assistants. He was looking for someone to keep a journal of his expedition and he liked my writing."

"*That is seriously flawed story, my dear,*" said Barry, sighing, and stuffing his ghostly pipe in his pocket. "*Think! Perhaps this Klost is truly a university professor. There is nothing that contradicts it so far, even if I have my doubts. Perhaps he does need to leave immediately for Brazil, why not? But then, why did he come directly from Bucharest to talk to you? Even a well-written article is a feeble reason. As our friend Terry pointed out, he could just as well have found someone in Romania. That would have been much simpler.*"

"What do you want me to say, Sir Barry? That is what he told me."

The ghost reflected. His brow furrowed. He took several steps, chewing his mustache. The four young people didn't move, watching that surreal scene of a dead sleuth pacing up and down the room, ruminating. He finally stopped and turned toward them, smiling, looking almost embarrassed.

"*You are right, young woman,*" he finally said. "*It is I who owe you an apology.*" He raised his hand to prevent any replies. "*Don't interrupt me. I am already angry enough at myself.*"

He took out his pipe, carried it to his mouth, and the bowl caught fire immediately.

"*At first, I thought you were an art thief, a kind of Raffles... These are certainly the type of gloves that a burglar you wear, but I now realize that you wear them to avoid contaminating the archeological sites that you have minutely cleaned with the help of those little brushes.*"

He drew a deep puff of smoke that spread out in a large opaque cloud around his head, still without any odor.

"*That leads me to a new conclusion, which will be, I hope, more accurate than my first. If those men came to steal from you, that was because, without knowing it, you have something that interests them.*"

"What is it?"

"*I don't know yet, my dear, but what is certain, is that they took a lot of risk, as so far as trying to kill you. So the object of their desire must be of extreme importance.*"

"What should we do next?" asked Mark.

"*Do you keep an inventory of all the items in your store?*" Barry asked Maureen, ignoring the young man.

"Yes, of course."

"*Then you must go back to your shop and check if anything has disappeared in your absence. Then we'll be able to determine a course of action.*"

"Which is what?" Mark broke in again.

"*Let's start with this, young man.*" Barry replied. "*You two go there by car, or train, or whatever means of conveyance you use these days, it doesn't matter, and return as soon as you can with the information.*"

"You're not coming?" asked Mark.

"Obviously not. He can't, Mark," said Maureen.

Angela got up to draw the curtains to let the light back into the room. The rays of the sun entered, filling the room with a warm aura.

"No need to stay in the dark, is there, Barry?" she asked.

"*Not in the least,*" answered the ghost. "*That's only ridiculous folklore. But it amused me to see your preparations.*"

"Why can't you go with Mark and Maureen, Sir Barry? Are you condemned to spend your afterlife in this room?" asked Terry.

Terry was never as much at ease as he let it seem. The presence of the ghost still made him feel uncomfortable.

"A ghost is confined to the place he haunts," explained Maureen, in a soft voice. "I doubt that our friend Barry can leave Tarford Manor, even he wishes to do so."

"*You are correct, young lady!*" said Barry. "*Even if I don't understand why, I always feel some kind of* barrier *when I approach the front door or an exterior wall. Only by going to the roof I can escape my prison—if only a little. I guess I am a prisoner of sorts here.*"

"Is there any way to free you? Some kind if spell, perhaps?" asked Mark.

"*Possibly, but that is not our concern right now. Have you decided, my friends? Do you want to find out who tried to kill young Maureen?*"

Terry, Mark, and Angela looked at each other briefly. It was Terry who spoke first:

"At the point where we are now, we might as well continue, no?"

8.

The preparations were rapid. The students didn't know how much time they had, or what they were going to find out. They also didn't know whom they were dealing with; obviously, men who were not afraid of taking drastic action, considering the length they had gone to with Maureen. They had never encountered a situation like this.

They decided that Maureen would go back to Ingersham, with Terry, and Angela. Mark protested, arguing that Maureen should stay safely behind at Tarford Manor, but he gave up very quickly when she argued that she was the only one who knew what as in her store. It was therefore imperative that she be part of the trip. Mark would remain behind, acting as liaison between them and the ghost. That decision made Barry smile; he suggested that they could take advantage of that time to get better acquainted.

An hour later, the trio left in Mark's car. There was silence, interrupted only by the directions given by

Maureen. Seated alone in the back street, Angela was thinking. In the space of less than twenty-four hours, her quiet student life had been turned upside down. She would never have imagined that she would find herself mixed up in such a fantastic adventure. Her life had seemed all laid out in front of her: her exams, success, marrying Terry, finding a job... And then, that fateful night had changed everything. Fate had put her on Maureen's path. Now, Angela had the impression of being a character in a movie. And what about Barry Barrison's ghost? That was simply unreal, unimaginable. If she hadn't been there when he first appeared, she would never have believed it. *Never*. However, she had to accept the incontrovertible evidence before her: there really was a ghost who haunted the walls of Tarford Manor, and with whom they had conversed.

That last thought brought a smile to her lips, because, as afraid as she had been, she had felt a tingling of excitement and a rush of adrenaline. She had touched the Uncanny, and liked it. It was too bad that neither Mark, Terry, or she could share that extraordinary discovery with the rest of the world. The existence of ghosts opened new perspectives onto the occult and parapsychology. She already saw herself imagined presenting an academic paper on the topic in front of a panel of erudite professors, leaving them astounded, just as Barry Barrison materialized before their very eyes. But it was too soon. Plus, she was not convinced that Barry would be willing to play his part. She had only met him a few hours earlier, but she was certain that the man, in addition to having a superior intellect and deductive mind, had a good dose of pride. Finally, it was not in her nature to exploit someone else callously. Besides, as Mark had suggested, the notion of being part of an extraordinary investigative team appealed to her very much. Perhaps their little group could look into other paranormal phenomena?

Maureen's voice seemed to come to her from far away. Angela looked outside the window of the car. They had been driving through the western suburbs of Greater London, sad and dreary as usual, for a good hour. She wondered: Did ghosts exist in the open countryside? They always seemed to associated with old dwellings, abandoned houses…

Angela shivered. She came out of her thoughtful reverie. A sudden thought made her gasp. She had just gotten the proof that ghosts existed, but what about other supernatural creatures? Vampires? Werewolves? Zombies? Witches? Were they all fantasies or a grim reality? The discovery of Barry's ghost had opened a breach into her perception of the universe, and that frightened her. Just like the shock of a first kiss, his arrival had propelled her and her friends into a universe a great deal more sinister than the one she had known until now. And she knew she would never be able to go back.

She panicked for an instant. She thought about asking Terry to turn around and hiding back in their flat. She would have gladly abandoned Maureen on the side of the road. She thought about cloistering herself in a church and reciting prayers to the Virgin Mary. She felt herself lost. Her chest rose and fell quickly. She had difficulty breathing. She felt an icy hand griping her shoulder. She turned around…

The frowning face of Barry Barrison was looking at her. His eyes were empty; nothing was there. His mouth was twisted into an anomalous smile. His mouth was open but no breath came out. Angela felt glacially cold. The odor of wet dirt submerged her. She could no longer feel her legs. She tried to move her feet, but in vain. She felt herself trapped again in the icy, muddy waters of the Thames, being dragged towards the bottom. She tried to cry out, but Barry's icy hand crushed her throat. The inhuman face of the ghost had now become an expression of savage fury. He tightened his grip. Angela felt the pressure of his fingers squeezing the life from her carotid artery. The pain was intense. She could no longer breathe. Tears flowed down her cheeks. Then, there was darkness.

"Take the first road to the right," Maureen's voice said.

Angela opened her eyes and took a deep breath. She put her hand on her throat. Nothing.

"OK," responded Terry.

The seat beside her was empty. No ghost. The circulation in her legs was normal. There was no smell. The young woman looked for Terry's eyes in the rearview mirror. He smiled at her.

"Well, well! Sleeping Beauty is awake."

He suddenly noticed her haggard look.

"Is everything all right?" he asked.

"Yes, everything is all right," she replied after a moment. "I was exhausted. I need some time to collect my thoughts."

"We'll be there in ten minutes," Maureen added.

Angela said nothing. Her heart was beating wildly and she was still short of breath. *That was only a dream,* she thought. *A bad dream and nothing more.* She finally got in control of herself.

She was still having trouble telling dream from reality. However, she now knew that her life had been changed forever.

9.

Ingersham was not the bucolic village one might have expected. Following Maureen's directions, they took a narrow street filled with potholes. The state of semi-dilapidation of the cottages bordering it made it a rather unattractive location.

"Jeez! Why did you decide to bury yourself in such a rat hole, Maureen?"

The young woman burst out laughing. She had been nervous and Terry's frank reaction did her good.

"Don't judge based on your first impression," she answered. "The rest is worse!"

Terry looked at her, his mouth open. Maureen laughed even more.

"I'm joking! That said, I was dubious too the first time I came here. I wasn't expecting something like this. The tourist office explained to me later that the village has undergone an astounding expansion and that the public purse was right, therefore, they had had to make some tough choices."

"This is an odd choice. How can a village prosper if its suburbs are dilapidated?"

"You are right. The decision was made by a small group of old people, who preferred to invest their money elsewhere."

The car went forward slowly. The houses seemed mostly abandoned. There were a few boarded up windows.

"Do people live there?" asked Terry

"Not many. This neighborhood is abandoned, or almost so. That is a part of the vestiges of the former village, dating back to the 1600. Go forward a little more and you will see. At the next intersection, take the street to your right. We will come to the *living* part of the town."

"Why the devil were those houses left abandoned?" Angela asked. "That's gloomy."

"You're right, but that was a decision of the local council."

"What's their excuse?"

"We don't have a proper mayor in Ingersham; a council of old men descended from the founding fathers have made all the decisions."

"Is that legal?"

"I don't know for sure, but I don't think so."

"Is this where I turn?" asked Mark

The car slowed down at the approach of the intersection. The new street seemed a great deal larger.

"Yes, turn right here."

Terry complied. They soon arrived in a more populated area and the change was radical. Angela let out a sigh. Her nightmare had left her queasy and she thought there should have been more people walking in the streets.

"Is this the main street?" Terry inquired, still perplexed.

"Yes," Maureen replied, and, anticipating the next question, she added: "I told you that there wasn't much of a crowd, even during the middle of the day. It's been like this for weeks. The locals don't come out until the evening."

"Why?" asked Angela, scrutinizing the shop windows.

"I don't know. I've been here only a short time..."

The ringing of Angela's mobile phone interrupted her.

"Yes, Mark? I'm going to put you on the speaker."

"*Hello, my young friends. Where are you?*"

Barry Barrison's voice resounded inside the car. Angela couldn't hold back a shiver. She passed her hand over her throat.

"We've arrived," answered Maureen.

"*At your shop?*"

"Not quite, we're only a few minutes away..."

"*Then I will talk to you when you are at your destination.*"

The call was cut off.

"That was rather rude!" commented Angela.

"He is not from our time, my dear," Terry teased. "He will need some time to adapt."

"After that white car over there, turn left," interjected Maureen. "That's Peacock Street, where my store is."

"You haven't even told us what its name is?" asked Terry.

"*Ye Old Shop*—not too original, I know," Maureen answered.

"But charming."

The car turned into Peacock Street. All around there were stores, some small, some big: a greengrocer's, a bakery, a tobacconist, a bank, a clothing store, a newsagent. Diversity wasn't lacking. But, here too, almost no one was walking about. They had hardly seen more than three locals, one of whom was a little old man pushing a shopping cart along.

"There!"

Maureen pointed her pretty finger at a big wooden sign suspended by a rolling chain to a wrought iron bar above the door of her shop. On it was painted in delicate cursive letters: *Ye Old Shop*. Terry had no trouble parking right in front of it: There were plenty of parking spaces in the street.

"This place gives me goosebumps," grumbled Terry getting out of the car. "I have the impression we're in a ghost town."

He was rejoined by the two young women.

"There's a back entry. I usually go though there," said Maureen.

Angela's telephone rang; the young woman answered and turned on the speaker.

"We're here, Sir Barry," she said.

"*I know*," answered the ghost in a dry tone. "*That's why I called you.*"

Angela made a sign of incomprehension to her companions. Terry shrugged.

"*You should go inside at once*," added the ghost.

"But I no longer have the keys," replied Maureen.

"*No need for keys. The door is open.*"

"How can you know?"

"*You have been burglarized, young woman. I hardly think that anyone would have taken the trouble to lock up afterward!*"

Terry looked right and left. No one was in the proximity. He placed his hand on the door knob and turned it. The door opened silently, setting off the welcoming bell. He stepped inside, followed by Maureen and Angela, who closed the door behind them.

10.

The interior of the shop was clean and well organized, smelling of waxed wood and furniture polish. There were shelves along the walls, on which were placed various items with a little easel in front of each with a card listing the price and origins of the item.

Maureen glanced around.

"Nothing seems out of place, at first sight."

She walked toward the left, giving several items a closer look.

"*Don't bother with the superfluous,*" thundered Barry's voice in Angela's telephone. "*Go directly to the inventory book!*"

"Why?" asked Angela.

She heard the ghost sigh.

"*Because, young lady, whatever the criminals stole, they were forced to look it up in that book in order to find it. There may therefore be clues, even perhaps a torn page, that will tell us where to look.*"

Maureen went toward the back of the room, passing behind a massive wood counter. She knelt down and disappeared from sight for a few seconds.

"The safe where I keep my inventory book seems intact!" she said, surging up from behind the furniture and depositing it a thick book on the counter. She opened it and began to flip through it.

Terry and Angela approached. Barry grumbled.

"*Are you certain, Maureen? Check closely, please. That is of the greatest importance.*"

The young woman continued turning the pages, one by one, checking carefully.

"I don't see anything out of the ordinary," she continued. "No folds, no page missing..." She concluded.

Angela expected a response, but nothing came. She checked that the communication had not been cut off.

"Sir Barry," she said, "are you there? Mark? Is anyone there?"

Terry shrugged, not knowing what to do. Mark's voice finally answered.

"We're still here! Barry is as still as a statue, right behind me."

185

"Be quiet, young man! I'm thinking! And cut off that infernal machine. Its noise bothers me!"

The line went dead.

"I believe our ghostly friend is pissed off," Terry observed, passing his hand through his hair. "It's not easy to work with a ghost, especially when he is as thin-skinned as this one seems to be."

He winked at Angela and turned back toward the shelves.

"Maureen, I'm impressed by what you're selling. It could be a Cabinet of Curiosities, such as the ones from the last century." He paused a moment, looking around. "I think it's a shame that all these objects are stored away in a little country shop. I think most of them would sell very well in a swanky London neighborhood."

Maureen, still leafing through her inventory book, shook her head.

"I have already been told that," she replied in a distracted voice, "but that doesn't really interest me." She closed the book and continued: "Definitely no page missing. No item has been stolen as far as I can tell. I don't understand…"

She came around the counter and rejoined Terry and Angela, who were examining the shelves.

"What are you doing?" she asked.

Angela examined her phone and placed it on the counter.

"Waiting for Sir Barry, I suppose," she said, sighing. "To be honest, this town makes me uncomfortable. Whatever we've got to do, I'd rather we did it quickly. I don't want to stay here any longer than necessary."

"On the other hand," Terry cut in, "let's remember that we left full of enthusiasm, following the advice of a ghost. To look for logic in a situation that was crazy

186

from the beginning is just compounding its absurdity." He paused, standing on one foot and then the other. "I don't know where all this is going, but I am like you, Angela. I have a bad feeling about this town. The sooner we leave, the better, I say. As for those who tried to kill you, Maureen, I fear they haven't yet revealed the full extent of what they're capable."

"What do we do, then?" asked Maureen, her voice trembling a little. "Sir Barry seemed so sure of himself."

Angela was fiddling with her phone as if expecting it to ring. She looked at her companion.

"You're right, Terry. That's madness. We should leave immediately."

"Wait," cut in Maureen. "Before we leave, I'd like to see if my car is still there."

She went behind the counter and started toward a door situated at the back of the store.

At the same moment, Angela's phone began to ring.

Suddenly, the back door opened violently. Maureen let out a cry of panic. Terry turned around and saw two armed individuals with dour faces. He had but a fraction of a second to avoid a shot from the one on the right. But he couldn't avoid another shot from the second man which struck him with force, knocking him backward. The young man's head hit the thick wood of the counter with a dull sound. He collapsed, groaning in intense pain, his sight blurred.

Angela moved toward Maureen. Paralyzed with fear, the young medium was totally still. The blonde girl stood beside her friend without really knowing what she would be able to do. Indeed, she didn't have time to do anything. One of the two assailants rushed toward them. Maureen screamed when the man slapped Angela.

To Terry's girlfriend, that slap seemed to last an eternity. First, she felt the rough hand against her cheek; then her head was forced to pivot to the right. The impact was so violent that she tasted blood in her mouth. Some red drops soiled the nearest wall when she turned slowly, like a broken doll. A second blow, to her shoulder, caused her to almost fall to the floor. She collapsed onto her knees, paralyzed by pain. Her knee caps made a sinister cracking sound at the moment of impact.

Angela lost consciousness. At the price of painful effort, Terry stood up, using his right arm to push himself off the floor. He wanted to check on her, but everything looked blurry to him and his reflexes were dulled. One of the men disappeared from his field of vision; the other one, who had struck Angela, had not budged, standing still with his legs apart. Terry didn't have either the time, or the strength, to avoid the foot directed right at his face. The impact was painful; his nose broke. Terry fell to the floor; an ocean of blood spread out around his face.

11.

"Be quiet, young man! I'm thinking! And cut off that infernal machine. Its noise bothers me!"

Mark obeyed. The ghost's voice had become glacial. His tone left no room for interpretation. He could almost feel the cold that emanated from him, standing behind him. The young man remained immobile for a moment, then turned around. Barry Barrison remained motionless, his gaze toward a fixed point, located on the wall facing him.

The ghost plunged his lifeless eyes into Mark's. He leaned toward the young man, bringing his face within inches of the young man's.

"*Something is not right!*" he finally said, after a moment. "*My deductions are no longer reliable. I made a mistake about Maureen's hobby. I identified her, wrongly, as a thief, and now her inventory book is intact!*"

He began to pace behind Mark's chair.

"*Mark Tarford! Nothing is going right at all in this affair. If Maureen's attackers were not trying to make her disappear in order to hush up the theft that took place in her shop, why then did they want to kill her?*"

He paused, frowning. He took his pipe out of his pocket and clamped it between his teeth. He concentrated and the bowl caught fire immediately. He began walking up and down again.

"I admit I don't have the least idea, Sir Barry," said Mark.

"*I don't doubt that!*"

"Then why ask me?" said Mark, annoyed.

"*A rhetorical question, young man.*"

Mark jumped up from his chair, clearly annoyed. He went around the table and stood in front of the ghost.

"With all due respect, Sir Barry, and despite the weirdness of your presence here, you don't impress me! Your condescension towards us and your inflated ego are unpleasant traits of character which stand out more than your alleged formidable analytical ability, which seems to have made your reputation while you were alive. I wonder if you're not just a bitter spirit, who lost his intellectual capacity, being condemned to wander the halls of this Manor forever? You sent my friends to that village based on a deduction that seems to have no foundation in fact," he continued, his accusing finger pointed at the ghost, who, impassive, said nothing. "You thought you had deduced a body of proofs that would lead to the truth!" He struck the table with an angry fist. "But in fact, the inventory book is intact. Nothing appears to have been stolen. What rabbit are you now going to take out of your hat to explain your failure? And what led you to deduce all this? Maureen wearing a medallion in the form of a little insect around her neck?"

"What are you talking about?" interrupted Barrison, suddenly frowning.

Mark, who was going to continue his diatribe, interrupted himself. He sighed; his anger lessened. He rubbed his eyes.

"I'm talking about that little necklace that she wears—a thin gold chain with a little pendant representing an insect."

"What insect?" asked Barry.

"How should I know? A little green thing with four or six legs, holding a little ball between its front legs."

A light appeared the ghost's dead eyes; had he been alive, Mark would have seen him turn pale.

"Call Angela immediately! They are in danger. Tell them to leave the shop—the town—right away. They must get out of there as soon as possible! To think I was doubtful from the start, like an imbecile!"

Mark dialed the telephone, trembling. He had not understood what had frightened the ghost, but a new sense terror knotted his stomach. This time, there was no arrogance in Barry's tone, just sincere fear.

Angela opened her eyes painfully. She was still in a daze. Her neck was sore. However, the melody she heard in the distance brought her out of her lethargy. That familiar and comforting sound pushed away the shadows. Was it a nursery rhyme? She was so confused. There were memories she couldn't quite grasp. Then she heard the ringing of her telephone. Everything came back to her: the men who had burst into the boutique, Maureen's cry; the short but violent fight; and the total darkness that had followed.

Angela clenched her teeth. Her knees were painful. She gripped the counter and managed to pull herself up at the price of some considerable pain and effort. Her telephone was ringing. She grabbed it with a shaking hand and weakly pressed the answer button.

"Mark?" she managed to say in a broken voice.

"Angela! Leave immediately! Don't ask me any questions. Just return to your car and leave Ingersham at once!"

The young woman looked around the room. The front and back door were open. A current of cold air hit her, making her shiver. She saw Terry's legs out from under the other side of counter. She cried out, dropped the telephone and rushed toward her boyfriend.

"Angela? What's happening?" shouted Mark's voice. "Angela? Are you there?"

Angela crouched by Terry, terrified by the pool of blood that had spread out around her boyfriend. Trembling, she put two fingers to his neck, trying to find a pulse. She searched several times, without success. Fear and tears clouded her vision.

She made another attempt. Then another…

Finally, she shouted: with relief and joy. She had just felt a faint pulse in Terry's neck. He was alive! She tried to turn him over. His face was bleeding, his nose was broken. He had been shot in the shoulder. He had lost a lot of blood, but was not dead.

Trembling, she stood up, looking for her phone through a curtain of tears pouring down her face.

"She's not there anymore," she managed to say, forcing herself to stay calm.

"Who isn't there anymore?" asked Mark.

"Maureen. We were attacked. Two men broke into the shop. They shot Terry and knocked me out, but Maureen's gone. Vanished. We need help."

Her voice faded off with a sigh.

"*Angela? Are you there?*" thundered Barry's voice.

Angela nodded silently.

"*Angela?*" repeated the voice in a softer tone.

"Yes, I'm here, but we need help—I beg you. Terry is wounded; my knees are hurt; I can barely stand. And I must have a concussion because I feel drowsy..."

"*I understand,*" *Barry replied, departing from his usual aggressive tone.* "*Mark is going to call the authorities on the other line. But I need one last effort from you, my friend. Maureen's life is at stake...*" He paused. "*Did you understand what I have just said, Angela?*"

"Yes, Sir Barry," replied the young woman who was trying to hold back her fear and pain. The effect of the adrenaline rush was starting to dissipate, and she was beginning to tremble throughout her whole body.

"*I need confirmation,*" continued Barry calmly. "*I must be certain that you understand. I need you to find a document, a manuscript, something like that in Maureen's affairs...*"

"Where should I look?"

"*Perhaps in the safe where she kept her inventory book? Or anywhere else where she would be likely to store that kind of document.*"

"Angela," Mark broke in, calmer, "an ambulance is coming; the police, too. I had difficulty explaining what happened; I had to, er, *adjust* our story somewhat, but they're on their way."

Angela went behind the counter and bent down toward the strong box. Its steel door was still open. It contained nothing, except a little jewelry box that looked damaged. She reported her find to the ghost.

"What's inside?"

Angela pressed the opener. It was empty. She told Barry.

"Do you see a desk? A filing cabinet?" he asked.

"No, Sir. There's nothing like that in the room. There's a drawer under the counter, but it contains only an account book, some cash, and some raffles tickets. Nothing out of the ordinary."

"Is there another room?"

Angela's headache was getting worse. The pain in her neck made it almost impossible for her to turn around. She pivoted slowly.

"Yes, there is a small closet."

"Is it open?"

"No."

"Ah! That may be what we're looking for! Quickly! We don't have much time. Open it and check out its contents."

The young woman did so. The closet door opened without resistance, revealing a tiny room with a little corner, a night stand, a chest upon which sat some ancient books, a little window and a sink in the corner.

"The books?" inquired Barry. *"What are they?"*

Angela glanced at the spines.

"Some novels, a book on architecture, and two treatises on mineral chemistry."

"Good Grief! Anything else?"

"No."

Angela left the tiny room. She felt a breath of warm air. Instinctively, she made her way towards the entrance, the door of which was still open. The wind stopped blowing. The atmosphere in the shop was oppressive, stifling. Suddenly, her gaze went over to a framed picture by the store window. She stopped and went toward it.

"I think I've found something, Sir Barry. I'll take it and bring it back with me."

She took the frame and pocketed it.

"I'm going to hang up now; I need to take care of Terry."

"The ambulance should be there in ten minutes," said Mark.

"Thank you, Mark."

The young woman hung up and went towards her boyfriend, who was still unconscious. She let herself slide slowly down and onto the floor, where she was found weeping by the EMTs.

A couple of hours later, sitting in the Regency Room of his Manor, Mark Tarford could at last examine the picture within the frame that Angela had grabbed, before being taken to the hospital with Terry.

It was a page from a diary written by hand. The paper was yellow, and the writing full of scribbling. However, it remained easily legible:

"...certain that it is necessary, despite our better instincts, to keep that tradition alive. It costs me so much, as it did each of my predecessors, to put in peril the jewel of our generation. But it is a necessary evil. Centuries of battles and preservation depend on it. The importance of the act must not be questioned. The Kheper is neces-

sary. And his ignorance must be total, for his own good..."

Next, there was a passage that was illegible, then the text continued.

"*...fragility can only be a strength. It is necessary to leave to aside the evidence in order to be certain to pass it on the next generation. In the past centuries, too many have failed...*"

There, a hole in the original document prevented the reader from deciphering the end of the sentence and what followed.

"*...only running water can be fatal to it. May he Ancient Ones make it so, ignored by those who would have it return.*

"*Never must you reveal any of this, and above all not to him, ever. Not until it is time. Then, he will know it. He will understand it.*

"*This jewel is the only thing which can thwart the inevitable. We know that well, and you shall you.*

"*They say that diamond is so hard it can break glass without even being scratched. May this one continue the tradition.*

Julius Antyphemus Clarius,
London, June 1921

Barry took a deep breath and turned towards Mark.

"*Young man, here is what we are going to have to do. I am going to ask you to give me all your attention. The lives, not only of Maureen, but perhaps a great number of people, depend on it.*"

Mark looked at the ghost. For the first time since their initial encounter, he looked at the ghost with great seriousness.

11.

195

12

The hours—the days—that followed were extremely chaotic. The little town of Ingersham was the theater of much unusual activity.

Many doors were broken down by the Police, and a great number of arrests were made. The tabloids screamed about the dismantlement of a dark mystic cult which had taken possession of the town and planned to spread chaos in the area. The TV reporters tried to tamp down some of the sensationalism expounded by their print colleagues, but the fact remained that the main questions remained unanswered: Who? Why? How?

The authorities were both diligent and thorough—which wasn't often the case—and kept a tight lid on the entire operation, so very little actual news filtered out, leaving the journalists hungry, pushing them to rely on various speculations, each one crazier than the next.

In the Regency Room of Tarford Manor, the ghost of Barry Barrison was seated in an old armchair near the fireplace. His legs crossed, he was puffing nonchalantly on his ghostly pipe. Seated in a semi-circle around him were Maureen Simpson, pale, but with a smile on her lips; Terry Edwards, whose head and shoulders were bandaged; Angela Lake, who was wearing a neck brace and a knee brace; and finally, Mark Tarford, who had eyes only for Maureen, whom he had been deathly afraid of losing for good.

All of them had been bombarding the ghost with questions. Barry raised his hand, requesting silence; then, he spoke:

"First, you should know that I am truly delighted that you are all safe and sound. My condition, and per-

haps my isolation as well, might have made me less sensitive to the notion of bodily harm, and I am truly sorry that I put you in danger with my suggestions."

"All's well that ends well, that's all that matters," observed Mark.

Barry frowned, then smiled and replied: *"As you said, young man."*

"Sir Barry, how did you arrive at your conclusions that enabled the police to rescue Maureen before she was sacrificed?" asked Angela.

There, Maureen could not hold back a shiver. Mark nudged closer to her and put his hand over her shoulder. The young woman relaxed and smiled.

"The correct conclusions, for once," said the young man.

The others froze, fearing the ghost's reaction, but Barry was content just to laugh.

"Mark is right! I agree with you that I did make a number of mistakes, but I assure you, my friends," he continued, sweeping the group with his glance, *"that it will not happen again."*

He took out his pipe and crossed his leg, placed his hands under his chin and closed his eyes.

"Since the beginning of this affair, I was skeptical that Maureen was an innocent bystander, but I was incapable of knowing why I felt that. I allowed myself to be carried away on some wild goose's chases and made some unfounded accusations, for which I humbly ask your forgiveness, Miss. It was obvious that you were a victim in all of this, but I thought that you had brought upon yourself the chain of events that took you to the bottom of the Thames."

"Where I would still be if you, Terry, and Angela, hadn't rescued me," cut in Maureen, her voice trembling.

"Exactly!" noted Barrison with emphasis. *"Fate— and personally, I have always despised the notion of Fate, considering it a subterfuge for the weakness of men—but I must now admit that, in the future, I shall have to revise that preconceived notion..."*

Here, the ghost interrupted himself for an instant, his eyes looking into the distance, before he continued:

"...Anyway, having discarded notion that you had stolen something that someone was trying to recover and punish you for that theft, I told myself that it had to be the opposite: you already owned something that some- one else wanted to steal, and they wanted to make you disappear before you could talk about it. It is evident that the visit of these strange men in your shop was linked to that. That's the reason I asked you to go back to Ingersham—to find out what they had stolen from you. I was convinced that that answer would allow me to solve the case..."

Barry stopped again, cleared his throat, and contin- ued:

"But once again, I was wrong! Nothing was miss- ing. No stolen object. I was definitely confused..."

"And I was very nervous," added Mark with a smile.

"I don't blame you, young man."

"Apparently, I mentioned some detail I had noticed that was instrumental in solving the case."

"Indeed! You're the one who put me on the right trail—and this time, definitively I shall explain..." He turned towards Maureen. *"Could I ask you to show us the pendant around your neck, please?"*

Surprised, Maureen pulled the chain, hidden under the neck of her sweater. She took it out gently, showing off the obsidian pendant hanging there.

"*Do you know what this is?*" asked Barry in a soft voice.

"An Egyptian scarab, I think," she answered.

"*Yes, but it's also more than that. Do you know from where it comes?*"

"My father gave it to me when I was twelve or thirteen."

"*Did he tell you anything in particular about it?*"

"No, not that I remember, except that it was valuable, and that I should take great care of it. And that I should never be separated from it for any reason."

"*And he was right! That's a kheper.*"

"A what?" the three students exclaimed at once.

"It's an Egyptian symbol, very old, meaning rebirth and protection of the living," supplied Maureen. "But what does that have to do with me?"

Silence filled the room.

"*That's what makes this situation so unusual, Maureen,*" said Barry. "*Because, in the end, that's why I understood that it was* you *that those men came to steal, not any artifact.*"

"Me?" asked the young woman, incredulous."

"*Does the name of Julius Antyphemus Clarius mean anything to you?*"

"Yes, that's the name of the man that wrote that old diary page that I had framed in my store."

"*Yes. And it's also the name of your maternal grandfather.*"

"My…???"

"*Yes, Maureen. And the jewel to which that diary refers is not any kind of earthly gem—it is you!*"

"I don't understand," said the woman, incredulous.

"*Are you originally from Ingersham?*"

"Yes, even if I didn't spend many years there. Some sad events made me leave at a young age."

"Why did you come back, then?" asked Mark.

"The shop. It belonged to my uncle. He left it to me after he passed away."

"What you did not know, nor did your uncle, was that, in willing you that shop, he put you in serious danger," explained Barry. *"Your grandfather was a part of a secret order that fought against a dark had its roots in Ingersham and planned to summon an ancient demon lord to sow on Earth. I'm speaking of a time when black magic and pagan cults were frequent in the English countryside. The founders of that order discovered amongst the relics brought back from Egypt a symbol that they decided to associate with a person dubbed the 'Jewel,'—the ultimate defense against the coming Demon Lord. A new 'Jewel' was appointed in each generation, with a magic rite being performed when the pendent was put on on him—or her."*

The young people remained speechless.

"Did you ever wonder why you had that old diary page famed?" asked Barry.

"Well, it's one of the oldest items that I found in the store when I took it over. It had been filed amongst various documents kept by my uncle. I found the writing pretty, even if I didn't understand much about the text. I thought it would make an interesting curio."

"That was a mistake, my young friend, that almost cost you your life. When these men—members of the Cult—came into your shop, and saw it, and then you, with that pendent hanging from your neck, they quickly deduced that you were the current incarnation of the Jewel, and it didn't take them long to figure out how to get rid of you."

"But why throw her into the Thames?" asked Terry. "Why not just kill her and bury her in a field outside Ingersham?"

"*Ah! That is where t gets interesting! According to the Cult's mythos, the* only *way to get rid of the Jewel is to drown him or her in running water—the living water of the Thames, which are sanctified by a Goddess, whose power alone can neutralize that of the Jewel. These lunatics have drowned Jewels before in her waters. They couldn't just kill Maureen; she had to be drowned in the Thames.*"

Maureen shivered. Angela could not help letting out a small cry. Terry remained with his mouth gaping. As for Mark, he tightened his grip around the young medium.

"So how were you able to figure out where they'd stashed Maureen the second time?" asked Terry.

"*By simple logic, my friend. I asked myself where the cult members could have gone. They could hardly plan another foray into London. They also had had to move pretty quickly. I therefore asked Mark to look for a place on the Thames, not too far from Ingersham, and somewhat isolated. The most likely choice was Preston Marsh. I took a risk, but fortunately, it paid off. What happened next, you already know. Mark alerted the authorities—the name Tarford still carries some weight in certain circles. Special Branch was immediately mobilized and the cult was dismantled—or at least, that section was. We don't know if there were an isolated community, or if there are more of them in other towns. In any event, the danger has been averted, at least for the time being.*"

"Am I safe now?" Maureen asked.

"*I can't tell for sure, but you may count on me to watch over you.*"

The ghost looked around the room.

"*Even if my range of investigation appears to be limited, at least for now,*" he finished with a smile. "*I'm leaving you. I have other matters to attend to.*"

The ectoplasmic form of Barry Barrison dematerialized, leaving the four students alone with their confused thoughts.

The Mystery of the Woman Who Walks

1.

Seated comfortably in his armchair with a high back, Barry Barrison was taking advantage of the calm of the night. It had been one of his occasional pleasures when he was alive, and he was glad that he could still enjoy it. He had been present, as a silent phantom observer, at the transformation and evolution of the British capital during all those years. Puffing on his pipe, he had been sitting for more than an hour, his legs crossed, his gaze lost in the distance, staring at the lights that lit up London's skyline, making it glitter. He was drawn out of his thoughts by a characteristic tingling in his head: a telepathic contact. He left his thoughts, although regretfully.

"*Yes, Angela?*"

"Sir Barry, sorry to disturb you," the voice in his head responded clearly, "but we need you to come and check out a video."

Barry Barrison rubbed his eyes, tired.

"*I'm coming.*"

"Thank you, Sir."

The contact broke off. Barry got up from his seat and looked for one last time at the perfectly clear stars in the heavens. With a mechanical gesture, he taped the bowl of his pipe against the terrace wall. As expected, nothing happened, and the object simply passed through the stone. After having placed his pipe back in his pocket, Barry disappeared, teleporting himself four stories down.

The Mystery Academy was based at Tarford Manor. It was composed of the four young people who had invoked the ghostly spirit of Barry Barrison a few years earlier, and had since developed a particular interest in mysterious cases that could not be solved by Scotland Yard, or other law-enforcement agencies. From a purely intellectual challenge at the beginning of their association, their interest had grown over a period of time, until they had decided to launch what they called the Mystery Academy.

Thanks to Mark Tarford's family fortune, the necessary renovations and updating of the Manor's facilities had been performed to their satisfaction. The young man had inherited the property, as well as his parents' considerable fortune, a few years back.

Barry appeared in the corner of the Regency Room on the ground floor, and, without saying a word, took his place in the comfortable armchair reserved for him next to the fireplace. Despite the chair's time-worn appearance, he had insisted that it should not be discarded. It was there, seated in that very same chair, his gaze lost in the hearth's glowing embers, that he had solved a good number of his cases. It had virtually become the only place where he could think.

He liked to repeat, to whoever would listen, that if Sherlock Holmes needed his violin to solve a case, he needed that armchair and the dying fire in order to find the solution to a case.

Barry looked at Angela Lake. It was she who was now the head of the Academy. The tall, young, energetic brunette was all that Barry would have wished to find in his own daughter, if he had had one. She was always eager to learn, never stayed in one place, and cared little about her physical appearance. She dressed like a boy, with clothes often too big for her, and tied her hair in a pigtail with the first rubber band available. Barry knew however that she could express her femininity very well when she took the trouble to do so, but her scientific personality cared very little about that.

The young woman was taking notes in a small ledger, while watching a video on a screen. Today, she was dressed in faded jeans, a heavy wool sweater with a turned down collar and sneakers. Her hair was held back in a compromise between a chignon and pigtails, certainly arranged cleverly to hold the ensemble at the back of her head. Her eyes moved constantly from the screen to her notebook.

Sitting at her side, Terry Edwards, on the other hand, seemed to have trouble concentrating on the video. He was Angela's fiancé and the practical man in their little group. Barry liked him for his lively mind and his dexterity with a camera. Angela, always the professional, managed to separate their lives as a couple from the Academy business. It wasn't always so easy for Terry.

Terry pointed at the images on the screen.

"I'm afraid the quality isn't very good," he said.

Angela glanced at him, half-angry, half-amused.

"Didn't you hear what I just said? That was taken with a cheap phone."

Terry passed his hand through his blond hair, scratching his head, uncomfortable.

"Oh, yes, I forgot," he said, uncomfortably.

"*What are we looking at?*" asked the ghost.

Angela jumped. She turned toward the ghost, who was seated in his armchair, his legs crossed, a big smile on his face, which made his mustache go up even higher.

"Sir Barry! You know how much I hate it when you show up unannounced!" she whined.

"*But, young woman, this is home, even if I am reduced to the state of a ghost and condemned to wander inside these walls for eternity. Even so, I have the right to go about however I wish.*"

"I'm so sorry; you're right, of course," stammered Angela

Barry stood up, adjusting a tweed jacket that had not left his shoulders for decades.

"*Come now, Angela, I was teasing you,*" he said with a smile. "*I know that you don't like my unannounced arrivals...*" He acknowledged Terry with a friendly wave. "*So, what are you working on that is so important that you summoned me via telepathy?*"

"This, Sir Barry," answered Angela, touching her keyboard. "This video was taken a few days ago by a group of French students. Look!"

She pressed a key. Barry concentrated on the images on the screen.

First, he saw the windows of the top floor of a dilapidated building. The video was jumpy, shook all over the place; a gaggle of confused voices could be heard in the background. The camera went from window to window, as if it were searching for something in particular. After a few seconds, cries were heard in the vicinity. The camera then stopped on the top window on the left of the building.

"Look! There! I was right! There really is a man up there!" said someone on the tape.

"No, you're crazy; it's a woman," answered someone else.

"What? That's a woman? Then, she doesn't have a particularly good figure!" replied the first person.

Several other voices, excited and shouting, mingled with the first two.

"Step back and let me film. I can't see anything!" exclaimed the first voice.

Several shouts of protestations erupted, but order was soon restored.

Barry frowned and stepped forward. He went through Angela and Terry, making them shiver a little, as he got closer to the screen. The picture showed, now a little more clearly, the window in question. Despite the poor quality of the image, and that lack of focus, he could distinctively see a human silhouette—a woman's—walking up and down behind the window. She was dressed in a light grey shirt, had long black, stringy hair. She was walking with difficulty, seemingly dragging her feet.

"When was that video shot, you said?" he asked without turning around.

"Three days ago, Sir," answered Angela.

"Is it authentic?"

"Yes, Sir," answered Terry. "It was taken with a cheap cell phone, and uploaded online only a few hours after being filmed. I doubt there are any special effects behind it."

"You doubt or you are sure?"

Terry squirmed about. "Well, one can never be one hundred percent sure, Sir."

"Then it could be a fake?"

"Yes, but I don't think it is, Sir," the young man finally answered.

There was a silence, during which Barry continued examining the feminine silhouette walking up and down behind the window. Around the cameraman, people were chattering non-stop.

"*What makes you say that?*" asked Barry.

"Well, if you look closely, you can see a reflection in the mirror behind the woman. That is something that would be very difficult to fake," Terry replied in a somewhat smug tone.

A big smile lit up Barry's ghostly face.

"*I'm proud of you, my boy!*" he declared.

Angela had the contrite face of someone who had missed a detail that she thought she should not have missed. She turned off the video.

"What do you think, Sir Barry?" she asked.

The ghost remained still, thinking, then he began to pace in front of the desk, lost in his thoughts.

Terry turned towards Angela, questioning her silently. The young woman shrugged. Neither of the two dared to speak. They were content to follow the ghost with their eyes, attempting to guess his thoughts. After a moment, which seemed to them like an eternity, Barry stopped walking.

"*Angela?*"

"Yes, Sir?"

"*You should leave tomorrow for France.*"

"Why so quickly?"

"*Because if what we saw is true, we are facing a situation that will soon require our intervention.*"

Angela smiled. She was delighted with the ghost's decision. It matched her intuition.

"Good," she continued, standing up. "Should I go alone?"

"*Of course not! You will need Terry's sharp eyes and Mark's ears. Take the first flight to Paris. After that, you'll proceed directly to... Where did you say was that video taken?*"

"Reims, Sir. At the Jean Jaurès high school, to be precise, "answered Angela, after having consulted her notes.

"*Reims, you said...*" For a moment, Barry seemed to remember something, but shook his head and continued: "*I have the feeling I am missing something...*"

"Terry, go find Mark and let him know about our departure tomorrow," aid Angela. "I'll take care of a few details with Sir Barry."

The young man got up, waved good-bye to the ghost and and left the room, closing the door quietly behind him. Angela turned toward Barry, who was still standing there, looking pensively at the blank screen.

"Any particular instruction for tomorrow?" she asked.

Barry turned towards her, his forehead furrowed. "*I don't know, dear girl. I don't know why there would be such a manifestation at this moment...*"

"I don't understand, Sir," Angela answered, visibly puzzled.

Barry moved about, waving his hand in front of his face, as if to chase away useless ideas.

"*It's normal that you wouldn't understand something supernatural,*" he answered. "*For the moment, you don't need to. The only thing I ask of you is to go there as fast as possible. I will expect a detailed report tomorrow night.*"

Without saying anything further, Barry suddenly disappeared. Angela remained alone with her thoughts. In spite of the affection she genuinely felt for the ghost, there were moments when he acted superior that she really resented him. She picked up her lap top and left the room, after having turned off the light.

2.

The next day, the three young people were in France. Mark had been enthusiastic about the trip. He was the valued third member of the Academy: Angela was the thinking head; Terry the irreplaceable handler and camera man; and Mark was not only the one who knew how to smooth things with authorities but he was also an excellent sound recorder and a proficient athlete.

After landing at Charles de Gaulle airport in the morning and renting a car, the trio had driven to Reims, where they had arrived in the early afternoon. Angela had rented two double rooms for Terry and her, and Mark, in one of the city's best hotels.

After checking in and parking their car, the trio had moved into their respective rooms. Mark set up the laptop and established a connection with Tarford Manor. Meanwhile, Angels was looking for the exact location of the strange apparition on a map, while Terry was checking his video equipment.

Soon, a window opened on the screen. The trio saw the ghostly form of Barry Barrison and, next to him, the red-haired curls of their friend, Maureen Simpson.

The pretty young woman was a gifted medium, and the fourth member of the Mystery Academy. She had been part of the group since its inception, having been rescued from a coven of devil worshippers.

"Maureen! Are you joining us?" Angela shouted.

"Yep!" responded the young woman with a big smile. "The connection is perfect."

"Good. We have arrived in Reims. We're at the hotel. I've identified the building where the video was taken; it is on one of the major thoroughfares. We plan to explore it around midnight. I hope that we won't be disrupted. Sir Barry, do you have any new information to impart?"

The ghostly silhouette moved behind Maureen's shoulder.

"*No, not at the moment,*" he answered. "*I count on you to be my eyes, and my ears tonight.*"

"Very good, Sir," responded Angela. "We will do everything in our power. We will make contact again after our first recon."

She ended the videoconference. Terry, seated on the edge of the bed, gave her a questioning look.

"What's happening? I feel that you're tense."

Angela sighed. "Yes, but I have a bad feeling about this business."

"Anything to do with Barry?"

"I don't know yet, but I am worried, that's all. He seemed unusually perturbed by that video yesterday."

"Perturbed?" said Mark, surprised. "But Barry is always perturbed. Maybe that's because he's a ghost?"

Annoyed, Angela replied: "You know what I mean! It reminds me of the state he was in during the Affair of the Camping Ground Mystery."

Mark sat back in his chair, scratching his head. "Sometimes, I think that you worry too much, Angela."

"I'm going to go down and get a drink at the bar," she replied curtly.

She turned around, grabbed her coat and left the room, slamming the door behind her.

"I think that you've annoyed her, Mark," said Terry, after a minute of embarrassed silence.

Mark got up from his chair and went to stand in front of the window. He looked down with an absent expression at the street below.

"Yes, I know, I'm sorry about that."

3

The Avenue Jean Jaurès in Reims was a large avenue named after the celebrated socialist leader. However,
at that late hour, there was little automobile traffic nor
many people passing through. The trio had left the Hotel
at about eleven o'clock. Angela, who had returned an
hour after her stormy departure, had decided that they
should go on foot. It was raining. Despite the street
lights, the avenue had that sinister look of city streets of
the early 19th century. It was bordered by tall buildings
with narrow windows, some with Venetian blinds, in rather dilapidated condition. Rain covered the asphalt and
the sidewalks with a fine layer of water that hurts the
eyes by reflecting the lights. In that part of the town, the
street lights were still equipped with the old yellow
bulbs that gave off a dull, unhealthy glow.

"What a dismal area!" Terry said. "It looks as if
we're in Whitechapel."

Mark silently agreed. They took refuge in the en-
closure of the enormous double doors that allowed entrance into the local high school.

The virtual recon made earlier by Angela allowed
them to locate precisely the window that was featured in
the video recording. It was in front of them, on the third
floor of a narrow building squeezed between two larger
buildings, one of them housing an antique shop. The
shutters on the two first floors were closed; those on the
third were not. In front of the entrance were several or-
ange cones used by the city workers to mark public
works.

"Let's begin," Angela said. "Terry, get the camera
ready. Mark, tell Maureen and Sir Barry that we're going
to begin our surveillance. I'll walk back down the street

to the north; Mark, you do the same to the south. Let's keep our headphones on so we can remain in contact."

The two men agreed. She started down the Avenue; Terry turned on the camcorder. As for Mark, he walked in the opposite direction, his hands in his pockets, looking for any suspicious signs.

He put his hand on his right ear where his ear piece was.

"Maureen? Can you hear me?" he asked.

"Perfectly, Mark," she answered in his ear.

"Terry just turned on the camcorder; you should be receiving the first pictures."

"*I hope that they'll be clear!*" Barry's voice resounded in the ears of the three young people at the same time. "*Because last time, it was hard to get all the details I needed to see.*"

"Don't worry, Sir," replied Angela, as she turned around the corner. "That video was shot by were amateurs; we're professionals, ."

"*I certainly hope so, young lady.*"

"The first pictures are coming through, Sir," interjected Terry. "I am walking towards the door. The entrance to the building seems closed to the public, if I can believe the traffic cones on the ground just outside."

In London, Maureen and Barry's eyes were glued to the images. Maureen had picked up a notebook and a pen, ready to write down every detail. As for Barry, he stood behind the young woman, his arms crossed, concentrating.

"I am almost there," said Terry, whose voice came clearly through the earpiece. "I'm going to focus on the door."

On the screen, Maureen and Barry saw the video stop on the large double doors dating back to the 19th century.

"Nothing to report," continued Terry. "Nobody in the street. I'm going to shoot the entrance in detail. Other than the cones in front, there's nothing else to indicate that the building may be condemned.

"*Take a picture of the name plates, Terry*," ordered Barry.

The camera moved about, then stopped on five buzzers on the wall to the right of the door. Terry zoomed in. Maureen picked up her pad and took down the names she saw. There were five buzzers, but only three had names.

"Now, I'll see if I can go inside," Terry's voice continued.

"*Slow down a little when you step across the threshold, will you?*" asked Barry, in a commanding voice.

"The workers who put up that door weren't very skilled. One of the hinges is almost coming out of the wall."

Barry frowned. "*Angela? Is there a church near you?*"

"Not here, Sir," responded the young woman, "but I saw one on the map about 500 yards to the south."

"*Mark?*"

"Yes, Sir Barry?"

"*You are walking south the avenue?*"

"Yes, Sir."

"*Go up to the church and tell me if you notice anything unusual.*"

On the screen, they could now see a heavy door handle. Terry's hand grabbed it and turned it without resistance.

"It's open! What should I do? Do I go in?"

"Not alone. Wait until I'm here," said Angela.

"*Don't wait out front, Terry,*" Barry said. "*Go back and wait for Angela, then take her by the arm and walk calmly away, just as if you were on a date.*"

Terry obeyed. Barry's tone of voice left no room for discussion. He closed the door, feeling a current of cold damp air. Then he went down the street, looking for Angela. The place gave him goose pimples.

Meanwhile, Mark was approaching the church.

"I'm almost there, Sir," he said when he spotted it.

"*Very good. Go in closer and tell me what you see,*" answered Barry.

The young man glanced around. "I don't see anything in particular, Sir. It is lit up, just for security. It's a magnificent building, with a large stained-glass window. There's a main entrance and two side doors. There's a parking lot in front, with some parked cars."

"*Do you see a cemetery?*"

"Wait a minute. I'm still too far away..."

In the radio one could hear the light breathing of the young man hurrying. Meanwhile, Angela and Terry had met and were slowly going down the avenue, pretending to be a young couple on a stroll. They were now within hearing distance of their companion.

"No, Sir, I don't see any cemetery," said Mark at last.

"*Is there anything unusual about the church?*"

"What do you mean by unusual, Sir?" replied Mark, looking all around.

"*If I'm asking you, it's because I don't know,*" replied Barry sharply, before becoming calm again. "*Mark, I do not see what you see. You must describe everything to me—especially if it looks unusual to you.*"

The ghost paced behind Maureen's seat. He put his pipe in his mouth, puffing nervously on it.

"I'm sorry, Sir, but I don't see anything unusual. There's a newsagent shop across the street—closed, of course, considering the hour."

Barry appeared satisfied with that answer.

"*Good, Mark, thank you. I have the information I needed. You can go and join you friends.*"

"Maureen?" Angela interrupted.

"Yes, Angela," the young woman replied.

"Did you see that car that went by? I swear it's driven past us three times already."

Maureen seemed embarrassed. "Er…"

"Yes?"

"Terry's turned off the camera."

The young man had indeed turned it off when he had left the building to go and join his girlfriend. There were no more pictures. Angela stared at her boyfriend.

"I'm sorry," he whispered.

"*Angela?*"

"Yes, Sir Barry?" said the young woman, forcing herself to remain calm.

"*That automobile? Did it seem to you to slow down?*"

"I didn't pay attention to it the first time. But yes, it seems to me that it slowed down on its subsequent trips."

Terry turned back the camcorder back on. Barry and Maureen could now see images of the badly lit Avenue. The rain was still falling. The reflections it caused made the picture hard to make out.

"*Terry, did you have time to take a picture of it before?*"

"I don't know, Sir," replied the young man.

"We're only a few hundred meters away from the building," said Angela. "Should we slow down and wait to see if it comes back?"

Barry thought for moment.

"*No, we don't have time anymore. Tarry and Angela, you will go inside and close the door behind you. Mark, find a discreet spot near the entrance. If that car comes back, then you can take a picture of it.*"

"Very good, Sir. We'll be in position in a minute."

They arrived back at the front of the building. Angela looked all around. The Avenue was empty.

"We're going in, Sir," she whispered.

Terry turned the door handle. They were hit by a blast of cold air coming from inside. He turned on his camcorder and they entered carefully, visibly tense.

4.

Angela shut the door behind them. The stifling sensation due to the almost poisonous darkness that enveloped them added to her discomfort.

On the other side of the screen, in London, Maureen also shivered. Behind her, Barry had become still and was looking at the images meticulously.

"I wonder if there are people who still live in here?" asked Angela, more to hear the sound of her voice than for information. It was unthinkable that anyone could have lived in the building.

"*Don't trust anything you see, Angela. Be rational.*"

"I *am* rational, Sir!"

A smile appeared on the ghost's face.

"*I know you are, Angela,*" he replied in a softer voice. "*Just because we saw three names at the door doesn't mean that this building is inhabited. Our eyes only perceive the surface of things. It is with the mind that we see deeper.*"

"On the other hand, I don't see any trace of work being done in here—despite these cones on the side-walk."

"*Very good, Angela!*" said Barry, pleased with her observation. "You are exactly right; there is no more work being done in that building than there is tobacco in my pipe."

"I found a good spot," said Mark's voice suddenly.

Angela jumped. "Have you seen the car?"

"No, not yet. I am twenty yards to the south. If it drives by, I can't miss it. Angela, do you remember the make?"

"I'm not sure. A Mercedes, I think, or something like that. It was grey."

"*Did it seem dirty?*" Barry interrupted.

"I didn't see it very well, Sir." Angela replied, while still following Terry, who was walking slowly to-wards the stairs which led to the upper floors. He was making a wide sweep in front of him with his camera. "But it seemed to me that it wasn't in good shape. Why do you ask?"

"*Simple intuition. Terry, what are the sounds around you?*"

"There isn't a lot of noise, Sir. Everything is quiet, *too* quiet, even. Since we came in here, I feel cut off from the exterior world..."

They had been walking up the large staircase which led to the first floor. Angela had put her hand on Terry's shoulder and was following him in sync with his steps. The young man felt ill at ease. He could not explain why, but he felt that those walls had been the silent witnesses of tragic events. However, he knew that Barry was relying on them. He took a deep breath and composed himself.

They came to the landing of the first floor. No light came out from under the doors. Everything was plunged into darkness and a leaden silence.

"Continue. These flats are vacant, as I had supposed. Don't waste any time here!"

The ghost's tone made any argument difficult. On the screen, the images followed one after the other. Terry was obviously getting accustomed to the oppressive environment, and his filming was becoming more precise and stable, to Barry's great satisfaction.

"There's the stairway that goes up to the second floor," whispered Angela. "There is no sound at all in this building. That is very unusual."

"Be calm, Angela," interjected Maureen in a tone that she wanted to be as reassuring as possible.

Suddenly, Mark's voice interrupted the conversation: "Sir, I see a gray Mercedes-like car coming down the avenue with its lights off."

"How many men are in it?" asked the ghost.

"I see two of them in the front, and there is probably a third one in back."

"If they stop and get out, what do we do?" asked Angela, panicked.

"My suggestion is that you hurry up and go straight to the top floor. We don't know how much time you have."

The two young people climbed the stairs rapidly and stopped on the last landing—the fourth floor. The cold there was worse and even more piercing, cutting through their clothes as easily as the edge of a knife cuts through paper. The landing had only two doors. The first was located near them, to their right. The other was further down a small corridor.

"That's not the door we want, Terry," whispered Angela, pointing at the first door.

"How do you know?"

"*By the orientation of the building*," cut in Barry. "*If you had paid attention to your movements, you would know that the door to your right looks toward the south—the back of the building. The door you want is, logically, the one a little further away to your left.*"

Angela agreed. They progressed with caution along the corridor, Terry directing his light toward the door that stood out clearly in front of them.

"Sir, do you see this?" asked Terry.

Barry's face came closer to the screen, going through Maureen's body without even realizing it

"*Yes, I do*," he confirmed. "*I suspected something like that. It was obvious that we wouldn't be the first to get into that apartment.*"

The door was partially open, and its lock was broken.

Mark's voice suddenly resounded like an alarm in Terry and Angela's ears. "Guys! The car stopped. Someone got out and is now approaching the building. Angela! Terry! Get out!"

Angela let out an involuntary cry. Suddenly, she heard sobbing—and those sobs came from behind the half-opened door.

"What do we do?" Terry asked, tense.

"We don't have a choice. Let's go in. Besides, I want to investigate the source of that sobbing I hear."

Meanwhile, Barry was pacing in front of the large video screen. Maureen heard him grumbling.

"*Mark, what's the man outside doing?*" he asked.

"He's looking right and left. He's coming up to the entrance. He's stopping right in front of the door. He's taking something out of his pocket—I can't see what. Ah, yes, it's a pack of cigarettes. He's lighting one. He's leaning on the wall next to the door. He's not going in!"

"*Didn't you tell me there were three men in that car?*"

"Yes, Sir."

"*Then, he may be waiting for them. Terry and Angela, what are you doing? For God's sake, you should be looking for a way out!*"

Instead, Terry gently pushed the door open. It silently pivoted on its hinges, revealing a room plunged in darkness that had been turned upside down. The place had been ransacked, but only recently. Angela and her boyfriend went inside. The dry, cold air, mingled with the odor of dust, hit them. After crossing the threshold, they had trouble breathing. The sobbing was still there, but in the distance and seemed stifled. It was difficult to locate exactly where it came from.

"Terry, do you smell that?" asked Angela.

"What?"

"*What do you smell?*" asked Barry, impatient.

"A slight smell of smoke," answered Angela.

Barry frowned. Terry swept the walls of the room with his camera. Nothing seemed to have been darkened by fire.

"Perhaps in another room?" he suggested.

"I don't think so," replied Angela. "I don't think there's been any fire in here—or anywhere else in that building."

"I can smell it too, now," said Terry. "we still need to look around."

The thought of the imminent arrival of several hostile strangers worried him considerably, and he was already looking for ways of defending themselves.

The next room was an even more indescribable mess. It must originally have been a drawing room, but there was nothing remaining standing. Chests had been turned over, their contents dumped on the floor and rifled through. The video camera passed over old photos tossed about randomly on the floor. Then it stopped on an old desk, turned on its side. Terry zoomed in. One could see the gutted drawers, sheets of paper with quick handwriting on them, spread around on the floor like so many leaves of an uprooted tree.

They heard the sobbing again. It seemed both near and far away.

"A second man is approaching the entrance," reported Mark. Once could hear the tension in his voice. "He's talking to the first man. They seem very agitated."

"*Are they arguing?*"

"I can't tell. I'm too far away."

Mark was increasingly nervous. He knew that if the two men went inside the building, Angela and Terry would soon find themselves in an uncomfortable position.

Meanwhile, the two young people continued with their investigation. They came to another door that led to the next room. The sobbing continued. Terry pushed the door with his foot, revealing a corridor at the end of which was another door. There was no window, adding to the feeling of oppression. The odor of burning became stronger.

"*Keep going!*"

Maureen reclined in her seat; she was surprised by Barry's aggressive tone. .

Terry and Angela moved down the narrow corridor. The young man made a great effort to keep the picture stable. His hands were trembling.

"The two men are moving towards the entrance!" reported Mark from the Avenue.

Terry put his hand on the door knob. Behind the door, the sobbing was growing louder.

"I'll try to create a diversion," announced Mark. "Angela, Terry, take advantage of it. I don't how long I'll be able to hold them off."

In truth, Mark Tarford had no idea how he could distract the two men. But if they got inside the building, his two friends' lives may be in danger. He had to act. He opted for the first idea that came into his mind. Something he had more than a passing experience with.

Drunkenness.

He came out from his hiding place and staggered on, singing at the top of his voice the first song that came into his head.

The sudden sound in her ear was hard to listen to, and made Angela grit her teeth in reaction. Barry, on the other hand, burst out laughing.

The two men who were walking towards the entrance turned around to look at the festive lunatic who had unexpectedly appeared on the Avenue, They exchanged a questioning look. After a moment of hesitation, one of two went inside, while the other turned to confront Mark.

The young man stopped singing.

"My diversion only half worked," he muttered rapidly. "One of them went in. It's up to you now to deal with him. Me, I'll take care of the one who remained outside."

He started singing again, pretending to be under the effect of alcohol.

Upstairs, Terry pushed open the last door. Angela grasped his shoulders tightly. In front of them, by the light of the moon that filtered softly through the window, stood the silhouette of a woman walking ceaselessly up and down the little bedroom. She was thin, old, and pale. Dressed in a worn out nightgown, her arms down, she crossed again and again the short distance that separated the two walls, sobbing constantly. Her long black hair covered her face and fell down on her shoulders.

Terry backed away before regaining control of himself.

In London, Maureen sat open-mouthed in front of the screen. Barry, his hands behind his back, was scrutinizing the image, frowning. He saw two little beds pushed up against each other to make a single bed, and an almost empty chest on which sat an old teddy bear and a few books.

The ghostly woman began to scream.

Outside, Mark threw himself at the thug that had come to meet him.

In the bedroom, the screaming woman looked at the young couple, staring at them with empty dark eyes. Maureen let out a cry of terror when the phantom's face disappeared, passing through Terry still holding his camera.

"Terry?" she asked. "Are you all right?"

"I... believe so," the young man responded.

He turned around. Angela was as white as a sheet. She also had felt the ghost going through her.

"She disappeared through the wall," stammered the young woman. "I felt her go right through me."

"*I have seen enough!*" interjected Barry. "*Get out of there, quickly!*"

The order struck the two young people like a whiplash. They turned around, and rushed back down the narrow corridor and the dilapidated rooms until they reached the stairs again.

Terry had been preparing himself to meet the second man who had come inside the building. They met him face to face on the first landing. Like a bullet, the young man delivered a direct blow to his opponent. The man staggered down, fell heavily, his head hitting several steps on the way down.

In London, Maureen and Barry couldn't follow the fight except through the chaotic pictures transmitted through the camcorder. The young woman nearly broke the pencil she was holding.

Some instants later, Terry and Angela rushed out into the night. They took long, deep breaths of the air outside. Despite the drizzle, it seemed to them as fresh as a spring breeze.

Barry relaxed. Maureen broke into sobs of joy when she saw the picture stabilize and heard Terry's voice.

"They're out!" she exclaimed.

On the other side of the Avenue, they saw Mark, out of breath, standing on top of the imposing bulk of the other man.

The three young people left the place as fast as possible. It was only after running for twenty minutes that they finally stopped to catch their breath.

A look behind them convinced them that they had successfully outdistanced the unknown men.

After the three friends had gotten back to their hotel, in the Regency Rom at Tarford Manor, Barry sat silently for a long while in his favorite chair, his eyes staring into the reddish embers of the chimney fire.

He had looked again at Terry's video, stopping at various points, rewinding, freezing frames, and zooming in on certain details. Maureen had long left the room to go to bed, after turning out the lights. His ghostly pipe in his mouth, the ghostly sleuth sorted out his ideas at the rhythm of his exhalation of smoke, his eyes fixed on the hearth...

5.

The next morning, just after sunrise, Mark's computer emitted strident sounds which woke him up. He, in turn, woke his two friends.

Looking at the news, the three of them immediately learned of the arrest of three German suspects, two of whom were bothers, that same morning in Reims.

Angela immediately contacted Tarford Manor.

"*Ah! Angela! I'm happy to see that you are well rested,*" said Barry, with a satisfied air, seating nonchalantly in his chair in front of the screen.

"Can you tell us what's going on, Sir?" demanded the young woman.

"*Of course, my dear.*"

"Well, we're listening," said Terry.

"*That case featured several interesting details right from the very beginning. Remember the odd hinges on the front of the building mentioned by Terry? At first, I didn't know what he was talking about, but after looking at the video, I knew: It was a* mezuzah."

"Really?" interrupted Angela.

"We should have thought of it," said Mark.

"*As you know, a* mezuzah *is a Jewish religious artifact that is found affixed to the doorpost of houses*," Barry continued, in a somewhat pedantic tone. "*For someone who is not of that religion, it may seem like some kind of hinge. That's why I was curious to find out if there was a church nearby and asked Mark to check it out.*"

"But what is the relationship between a Christian church and a house visibly inhabited by Jewish folks?" Mark asked.

"*None, precisely. That's why I wanted to be certain that the place of worship you saw was indeed a Christian church and not a synagogue. The description that you made left me with no doubt. The presence of that* mezuzah *in that neighborhood was therefore unusual.*"

Angela rubbed her eyes, confused. "What about the car and its occupants?"

"*Reims was occupied by the Germans during World War Two. I theorized that, if someone was looking for something in that building, and in that flat in particular, it was possible that it could all be connected to something that had happened there during the War to a Jewish family. This line of reasoning was bolstered by the fact that the car in question was a Mercedes and looked dirty because it had been driven for several hundred miles.*"

Terry sat down on the bed. "I suppose that makes sense. What about the odor of burning? What did you deduct from that?"

Barry uncrossed his legs and, with a pensive air, puffed on his pipe.

"At this stage, I had a hypothesis, but I needed confirmation. The smell of burning you reported made me think I was going in the right direction. A mummified body can let off a similar smell to that of smoke. But just one mummified body would only put off a rather feeble odor. For you to have smelled that odor in that flat meant that you were either very near a body—but your camera showed nothing of the kind—or that there were a number of bodies hidden nearby. But what would mummified bodies be doing in that flat? And why hadn't anyone noticed them before? The answer was obvious: it was because they had been cleverly hidden..."

Angela, in her turn, sat down on the edge of the bed. "But why? And by whom?"

Barry sighed and smiled sadly at the young woman.

"That is the whole drama of that tragic story. Think of the photographs thrown on the floor, the two little beds in the bedroom, the teddy bear..." He stopped an instant, then continued: *"The photographs showed a family of five, a woman with four little children with a yellow star pinned on their jackets. They were smiling, their Mama standing behind them. Do you remember the names missing on the buzzers downstairs? I did some research and found the history of that woman, reported, somewhat incompletely, of course, in the local newspapers of the time..."* Here, he paused again, visibly troubled. *"She was a woman who had to endure the violent temper of her husband, a notorious alcoholic who, one night, when he was drunker than usual, indulged in his favorite pastime, beating his wife. A violent altercation took place in the kitchen. As she always did when that happened, the woman told her children to go and hide in*

a secret closet in the bedroom while her husband's anger lasted. But that one night, the blows were so violent that the woman feared for her life. To save herself, she pushed back her husband who was charging her with a kitchen knife. Under the force of the blow, the husband went through the window and fell into a back alley behind the building. As bad luck would have it, a German patrol car was passing by. They arrested the poor woman and later deported her. Her final fate remains uncertain, but there's no doubt that she died in the death camps."

"What about the children? "Angela asked in a trembling voice.

"They could never leave that secret closet. They perished, locked up, all four of them together."

"But, Sir, how did those Germans find that apartment? And what is the connection between them and that poor woman?" asked Terry, his mouth dry from emotion.

"When the police arrested these three men, one of them was found in possession of an old diary written by a German SS who was there the night in question, In his diary, the man recounted that he had heard the children screaming for help, but had laughed and left them purposefully to die slowly and painfully. One of those arrested was the grandson of the SS, and he sought to erase the traces of the infamy of his ancestor's conduct. It is at that point that the ghost of the children's mother manifested itself."

A long silence followed, broken only when Barry continued.

"At my behest, Maureen immediately contacted the French authorities. Right now, the remains of the children are being recovered and will be given a proper fu-

neral. The three intruders, who broke into private prop-erty, will be extradited to their country, which will de-cide their fate. You can come back home, my young friends. You have acted brilliantly."

Barry cut off the connection. Mark, Terry and Angela remained silent for a long moment before they started gathering their personal items.

It was only when they were on the plane back to England that they felt comfortable enough to talk about the affair.

HEXAGON COMICS CATALOG

Bob Lance #1: The Round Table. Carpi & Bernasconi. 64 pages b&w. $12.95.

Bob Lance #2: To Seek the Holy Grail. Carpi & Bernasconi. 54 pages b&w. $12.95.

Bob Lance #3: The Ghost of Rasputin. Carpi & Bernasconi. 54 pages b&w. $12.95.

C.L.A.S.H. Frescura & Trevisan. 248 pages b&w. $20.95.

Dick Demon: Vanishing Point. Lofficier, Arden & Peniche. 108 pages color. $26.95.

Dragut/Scarlet Lips. Lofficier & Macall. 68 pages color. $19.95.

The Enchanters. Lofficier, Mayorga & Castro. 88 pages b&w. $12.95.

The Frontiersmen/Codename: Glory. Lofficier, Peniche & Mayorga. 48 pages b&w. $9.95.

Galaor, Warrior of Mû. Lofficier, Macall, Xavier & Peru. 68 pages color. $19.95.

Guardian of the Republic #1. Mornet & Roncagliolo. 48 pages color. $12.95.

Guardian of the Republic/Barbarella. Lofficier & Ruiz. 48 pages color. $12.95.

Guardian of the Republic/Dragut/Scarlet Lips/Time Brigade. Lofficier & Macall. 48 pages b&w. $9.95.

Guardian of the Republic/Kit Kappa/Night Prince. Lofficier, Castro & Garcia. 48 pages b&w. $9.95.

Guardian of the Republic/Phenix/Super-Patriots. Lofficier & Macall. 48 pages b&w. $9.95.

Gun Gallon. Lofficier, Macall & Picard. 48 pages b&w. $9.95.

HEXAGON COMICS: THE FIRST 70 YEARS. Lofficier et al. 300 pages b&w. $22.95.

Hexagon Group #1: The Dark Hive. Lofficier, Roncagliolo & Ruiz. 76 pages b&w. $12.95.

Hexagon Group #2: Hexagon vs. Heptagon. Lofficier, Roncagliolo & Garcia. 96 pages b&w. $12.95.

Hexagon novel #1: Dark Matter. D'Huissier. 300 pages. $22.95.

Hexagon Spotlight on Alfredo Macall. 68 pages color. $19.95.

Kabur #1. Legrand, Lofficier & Bernasconi. 252 pages b&w. $20.95.

Kabur/Zembla. Lofficier & Ratera. 84 pages color. $24.95

Kidz. Lofficier & Macall. 52 pages b&w. $10.95.

The Lunatic Legion. Lofficier, Bouquet & Lafuente. 52 pages b&w. $10.95.

Morgane. Lofficier & Lirussi. 48 pages b&w. $9.95.

The Partisans #1. Thomas, Lofficier & Guevara. 48 pages b&w. $9.95.

The Partisans #2. Lofficier & Guevara. 64 pages b&w. $12.95.

Phenix #1. Lofficier, Bernasconi & Roncagliolo. 248 pages b&w. $20.95.

Scarlet Lips: Crimson Dawn. Wolfman, Lofficier & Guevara. 48 pages b&w. $9.95.

Starlock/Homicron. Lofficier & De La Torre. 54 pages color. $14.95.

Strangers Origins: Homicron. Buffolente, Lofficier & Dzialowski. 364 pages b&w. $24.95.

Strangers Origins: Jaydee. Grossi. 260 pages b&w. $20.95.

Strangers Origins: Starlock. Legrand & Bernasconi. 256 pages b&w. $20.95.

Strangers #0: Omens & Origins. Lofficier & Various. 128 pages color. $29.95.

Strangers #1: Strangers in a Strange Land. Lofficier & Various. 160 pages color. $34.95.

Strangers #2: Of Blood and Fire. Lofficier & Various. 160 pages color. $39.95.

Strangers #3: Of Gods and Men. Lofficier & Various. 160 pages color. $39.95.

Strangers #4: The Coming of Starcyb. Lofficier & Various. 118 pages b&w. $12.95.

Strangers #5: The Kingdom of Shivar. Lofficier & Peniche. 94 pages b&w. $12.95.

Tales of the Hexagonverse #1: Mutations (anthology). D'Huissier ed. 244 pages. $20.95.

Tales of the Hexagonverse #2: Family Business (anthology). D'Huissier ed. 244 pages. $20.95.

Tales of the Twilight People: Dr. Despair. Lofficier & Agapit. 148 pages b&w. $12.95.

Tiger and The Eye. Lofficier & Ruiz. 136 pages b&w. $12.95.

The Time Brigade: The Grail Wars. Lofficier & Green. 48 pages color. $12.95.

Wampus #1. Frescura & Bernasconi. 232 pages b&w. $20.95.

Zembla #1. Oneta & Oneta. 280 pages b&w. $22.95.

TO ORDER: Add $4 first bok, $2 for subsequent books, for p&h. Pay by credit card/paypal direct from our website: *www.hexagon.comics.com/shop.html*

or pay by check to the order of BLACK COAT PRESS sent to: BLACK COAT PRESS c/o Mr. Greg M. Seigel, 18321 Ventura Blvd., Suite 915, Tarzana, CA 91356.

E-MAIL INQUIRIES: info@blackcoatpress.com.